S0-CFG-238

ALSO BY ALLISON VAN DIEPEN

Street Pharm

Snitch

RAVEN

ALLISON VAN DIEPEN

SIMON PULSE

NEW YORK LONDON TORONTO SYDNEY

This book is a work of fiction. Any references to historical events, real people, or real locales are used fictitiously. Other names, characters, places, and incidents are the product of the author's imagination, and any resemblance to actual events or locales or persons, living or dead, is entirely coincidental.

SIMON PULSE

An imprint of Simon & Schuster Children's Publishing Division
1230 Avenue of the Americas, New York, NY 10020
First Simon Pulse paperback edition February 2010
Copyright © 2009 by Allison van Diepen
All rights reserved, including the right of reproduction in whole
or in part in any form.
SIMON PULSE and colophon are registered trademarks of Simon & Schuster, Inc.
Also available in a Simon Pulse hardcover edition.
For information about special discounts for bulk purchases, please contact Simon &
Schuster Special Sales at 1-866-506-1949 or business@simonandschuster.com.
The Simon & Schuster Speakers Bureau can bring authors to your live event. For
more information or to book an event contact the Simon & Schuster Speakers
Bureau at 1-866-248-3049 or visit our website at www.simonspeakers.com.
Designed by Paul Weil
The text of this book was set in Garamond.
Manufactured in the United States of America
2 4 6 8 10 9 7 5 3 1
The Library of Congress has cataloged the hardcover edition as follows:
Van Diepen, Allison.
Raven / Allison van Diepen. — 1st Simon Pulse ed.
p. cm.
Summary: New York City breakdancer Nicole loves fellow dancer Zin,
who harbors a dark secret.
ISBN 978-1-4169-7899-2 (hc)
[1. Friendship—Fiction. 2. Love—Fiction. 3. Magic—Fiction. 4. Immortality—
Fiction. 5. Break dancing—Fiction. 6. New York (N.Y.)—Fiction.] I. Title.
PZ7.V28526Rav 2009
[Fic]—dc22
2008025269
ISBN 978-1-4169-7468-0 (pbk)
ISBN 978-1-4391-5657-5 (eBook)

To my mother, Georgina Fitzgerald,
for more reasons than I can name

ACKNOWLEDGMENTS

I would like to thank Michael del Rosario, editor and former hip-hop dancer, for his enthusiasm and insight, and the wonderful teams at Simon Pulse and Simon & Schuster Canada for their support.

My love and appreciation to my parents; Sarah, Jeffrey, and Claire; and "G." A special thank-you to my husband, Jeremy, for his endless support during the writing of this book.

DYING
EMBER

Ask me the exact moment I fell in love with Zin, and I'll tell you it's the first time I saw him dance.

If you've seen him dance, then you understand.

If you haven't, then trust me—there's nothing he can't pull off on the floor.

Ask him why he isn't dancing backup for some big-name star, and he'll say he doesn't do anyone's choreography but his own, plus he's happy as hell working the bar at Evermore. It's the sickest club and ripest breaker battleground in Manhattan. He can't believe he actually gets paid when he'd be there anyway.

When Zin is working the bar, he's everywhere at once, just like on the dance floor. He wears black tanks and low baggy pants belted with clunky silver chains. He's an Arabic kind of beautiful, with short black hair and green eyes. His olive skin is pale from lack of sunlight, since he's mostly a nocturnal creature. He rarely goes to bed before six a.m., rarely wakes up before two p.m.

You should have seen Zin's face the first night I showed up to work.

"Carlo *hired* you? When did this happen?"

"Yesterday. Aren't you happy?"

"Yeah, of course." He wraps those lean, muscular arms around me. "Are you sure?"

My knees weaken at his breath against my ear. God, he smells good, like Ivory soap and aftershave. "Why wouldn't I be?"

"Don't you have to do homework or something?"

"College applications have already gone out. I'll only be working here on weekends anyway."

"Your call." He smiles that leonine smile. "I hope you're ready for some serious cash."

Evermore's home is a converted church. According to Zin, the place was gutted by fire six years ago. The elderly congregation, mainly from nearby Little Italy, couldn't afford to rebuild, so they joined another several blocks away. Carlo bought the place soon after, and now what was once a sanctuary holds a huge dance floor, velvet lounging areas, and tea-lit alcoves. He also restored the balcony, a perfect place to make out in privacy or spy on the action below. He left the surviving stained-glass windows as is, partially blackened by the fire, giving the place a gothic feel.

It's just before ten and the place is pretty deserted. DJ Gabriel's acid jazz echoes a hollow bass. There are two couples here on first dates; I can tell because the guys are trying not to look at my legs. (After a few dates, most guys allow themselves a look.) One of the guys is drinking heavily, and the girl is slapping off his hands. The other date is going well—the girl is in his lap already.

"Battle at midnight. I hope you have clothes," Zin says as he's fixing the drinks.

"I do, but I haven't asked Carlo if I can take a break then."

"He'll let you. He knows the dancing brings in customers."

"Who's coming?"

"Spinheads."

"Seriously?"

"Of course." Battling is the one thing Zin never jokes about.

"We'll do the new routine?"

"Yeah." He pauses, and I can tell he's going over the choreography in his head. "You're gonna do a dizzy run—end it with a buttspin. Then some applejacks while Slide and I are crabbing."

"Got it."

He loads the drinks onto my tray. "Don't forget to share your tips."

"Yeah, right."

He laughs and slides down the bar to a customer.

Just before midnight the rest of the Toprocks show up: Slide—tall, lanky black kid; Rambo—short, spiffy Puerto Rican; and Chen, who's got the muscular build of a gymnast thanks to intense training and protein powder. They're all

3

Brooklyn born and bred, except for Zin. And we're not only a breaker group, we're BFFs.

I want to warm up with them, but I figure I'll wait until the Spinheads show up before asking Carlo if I can take my break.

Turns out they don't show up until twelve thirty. By then Evermore is packed, a blazing sanctuary of dancers.

The Spinheads know how to make an entrance. They're wearing lime green tracksuits over purple tanks. We're not impressed. We don't need to follow some old-school dress code to know we're breakers.

"Can I take a break to battle? The Spinheads are here."

Carlo nods. Black-haired and thirtyish, he's known for his Gucci suits, unplaceable accent, and business savvy. "I look forward to it."

"I've only been training a few months. I'm still pretty much a beginner."

"We shall see."

I like the way he says it; I don't know why. Carlo seems like a strict boss, but deep down, he's really cool—Zin said so himself.

I change into some leggings, then hit the dance floor.

It's no surprise that Chen starts the battle by backsliding in front of the Spinheads and making angry hand gestures. The crowd forms a circle, and Chen begins with some toprocks.

Then he drops to the floor and spins on his hand. From there he breaks into a jackhammer.

The crowd cheers. Chen hoists himself into a handstand finish, slowly opening his legs. Zin runs up and front-flips over him. They move back and wait for the rebuttal.

Jam and Spinman jump into the middle together, locking arms back-to-back, with Spinman flipping over Jam's back and taking over the floor with a series of L-kicks. I see Zin and Chen exchange a look—it's a new move for Spinman.

Zin gives me the signal and I'm in with a dizzy run, adrenaline giving me an extra kick of energy. I finish with a buttspin. I back away, and Zin hits the floor, starting off with a few knee drops, then twisting into a headspin, after which he crabs around with Slide, weaving through his legs while I'm doing applejacks. Then Zin is doing airswipes, kicking his legs high in the air as the crowd cheers him on.

How can anyone rebut *that*? Zin is an Olympic athlete on the dance floor. No one can match him.

The Spinhead girl comes out with two steps. She's not bad. Her teammate T-Rex jumps in with six steps before lifting himself into a flare and finishing with an airtrack. His execution is flawless. I don't dare look at Zin's reaction.

Chen's back in, kicking his legs and twisting his body in a mobile skyscraper. Next, Rambo does some robotics. They pull back, and Zin leaps in with an aerial flip. He drops into a windmill, then pops up and flips onto his back.

For the final retaliation, Spinman does handless headspins called halos. T-Rex and Jam drop and start doing halos on either side of him. Their synchronization is awesome. Then, one by one, they each freeze in a different pose—a head freeze, a side freeze, a back freeze.

The crowd wilds out.

Damn it! They've won.

Zin throws up his hands and stalks off the dance floor. Chen looks like he wants to start something with Spinman, but Slide talks him down. He doesn't see that Rambo has got his hands on an empty beer bottle. I grab Rambo's arm, tell him to put it down. I don't know why Rambo always wants to fight. He's such a nice kid most of the time.

Electricity still in my blood, I dance for another minute. And then I feel it: I'm being watched. Not by groupies, not by breakers, but by my boss.

He's leaning against the bar, all dapper black suit, all class. He curls his index finger.

I go up to him. "Sorry I took so long."

"It's all right." His eyes focus on my hair. He gently brushes a lock out of my eyes. "You dance well, Raven."

Carlo has eyes so black you can't tell the pupils from the irises. It occurs to me that if I were ten years older, and if I weren't in love with Zin, I might be interested in the mystery behind those eyes.

I approach customers and start taking drink orders. I like that he called me Raven. I like the darkness of it.

I have a teardrop pupil in my left eye. It is exactly what it sounds like. My friends used to say it looked like my pupil leaked and the spill was contained in the iris.

If my eyes were brown like my dad's, instead of blue like my mom's, it would be less noticeable. But I'm not that lucky.

When I first meet someone, I often suspect they're staring at my pupil. Of course, it's hard to tell, since people are *supposed* to look you in the eye. If I'm going somewhere new, I sometimes wear dark brown contacts. It saves me from having to wonder what they're really looking at.

It doesn't matter, because when people look into your eyes, they don't really see you, anyway.

NAMELESS

My house is haunted by a ghost that isn't dead.

It might have been easier if he were dead. At least then we could remember him in the good days, the days of potential.

Mom hates it when I talk like that. She lives in hope.

Dad doesn't. He's a realist like me. He knows hope is a sham, at least when we're talking ghosts.

The house is quiet now. The ghost used to love loud, throbbing music bouncing off his bedroom walls. Me, I always preferred my earbuds, the music up close and personal. Now the only sounds are the low buzz of CNN or one of Dad's sci-fi shows.

The last time I saw the ghost, I spotted him in Chinatown in the early hours of the morning, smoking weed on a street corner with a white trash girl with dreads. I hadn't seen him in months. He looked different, worse. A long cargo jacket several sizes too big. Ripped jeans hung off him. He had a goatee of shaggy carelessness, the look of anarchy.

My feet hesitated. Should I stop? Or keep walking? The ghost didn't see me. My feet kept moving.

Zin saw that something had got me spooked. "Nic? You okay?"

"Shhh."

The first day of a semester is always the same.

Teachers see my last name. They ask about him, what he's up to these days, expecting big answers. I tell them he's doing fine, working.

What about Columbia?

He's taking some time off. I shrug like it's no big deal.

And they are confused, because the ghost never did things halfway, never took breaks. He graduated with a 4.0. They remind me of this when I hand in any assignment that isn't an A. I rarely do.

"How many days of high school left?" Chen asks.

"Ninety-two," Slide answers.

"That can't be right. You said eighty-seven last week."

"I wasn't including exam time. Now I am."

"Fine, but I hope the days start going down soon, because I don't know how much longer I can stand this hellhole."

Kim Tran, Chen's girlfriend, pats his arm. "Poor Chenny Wenny."

In senior tradition, we skip the cafeteria and eat lunch next to our lockers. We're all noshing on raw veggies out of mini Ziploc bags. Slide is into the raw food craze, thinking it'll boost our immune systems and give us an edge on the dance floor. It's better than Chen's suggestion last month that we do protein shakes twice a day. I'm not exactly going for the muscle chick look.

I turn to Slide. "You handed in your Lit paper, right?"

He nods. "Finished it on the bus this morning."

"Good." Slide needs a kick in the ass now and then. He's gifted ADD—too smart to be interested in his classes, too hyper to focus on one thing for long. It's not a recipe for high marks, but excellent for a breakdancer.

"Forty-six days till early acceptance," Slide says. "Nic, you're gonna be the first to find out. I bet you'll get in everywhere."

"We'll see."

"C'mon, you and Kim got nothing to worry about," Chen says. Being the spawn of two accountants, he's inherited a brain, he just doesn't use it enough, as most of his teachers point out. He's not worried about it, though. He fully expects that Kim will support his dancing career one day.

"Well, I don't have much extracurricular," I say. Everyone knows you need extracurricular for scholarships, and I doubt being part of a breaker crew counts.

My friends don't know that a ghost bleeds my parents dry. They don't even know that he's become a ghost.

11

My cell phone vibrates in my pocket. It's got to be Zin. It's 12:43—he woke up early today.

It's a text message.

HEY NIC
HOPE YR DAYS GOIN GOOD.
DONT 4GET PRAC 2NITE 730.
CU
Z

Kim pokes me. "That from Zin?"

"Yeah, just a reminder about tonight's practice."

"He never sends *us* reminders," Chen says. He leans over my shoulder. "Ooh, he's wishing you a good day. I swear you guys are dating behind our backs."

I wish.

"Keep going, Nic! Go, go, go!"

I swing my legs around in a coffee grinder, faster and faster, until I'm in the zone where I'm just spinning, weightless.

I stop on a dime.

The guys cheer.

Slide pauses the music. "That was sick! Since when did you get that fast?"

I pick myself up from the mat, blood rushing in my ears.

"Downed a double shot of espresso before practice."

"Red Bull's better." Slide unpauses the music as Zin hits the mat with spinning headstands. His legs thrust out in a V, and I can't help but notice his gym shorts falling back to reveal a serious amount of muscular thigh. Damn. Another thing about caffeine kicks—they make me extra horny.

Zin gets to his feet, his long black eyelashes spiked with sweat. "We gotta wrap soon, guys. I'm working later."

"I wish I could work on weeknights," I say.

"You're lucky, Nic. Carlo doesn't usually let people just do weekends. Guess he likes you."

"Well, I haven't spilled anything in a customer's lap—yet."

We usually practice twice a week, not to mention the actual breaking at Evermore on weekends. Zin formed the Toprocks a couple of years ago after putting up posters at a few dance clubs and holding auditions. Spinman was part of that initial group, but he and the other guys butted heads a lot, so he eventually defected and started the Spinheads.

The Toprocks didn't want to take on a girl back then. Even Chen and Slide, who knew me from school, questioned my intentions. They thought I was a groupie turned wannabe breaker, and at first, they were right. I thought taking up break-dancing would get me more time with Zin. Hell, I had no moves back then. I didn't even know I had them in me.

Zin showed me that I did.

I fell in love with Zin and with dancing. It's all one and the same.

The Toprocks warmed up to me soon enough. I earned my spot in their crew through countless hours of training with instructional DVDs, a mat, and an iron will. Turned out that having a girl breaker in the group—one who could really dance and wasn't a prop—was good for our street cred.

True, I have some limitations they don't have. I don't do headspins because I don't have the confidence or a spare neck if I break mine. I dance hard, but I'm not a risk taker like they are, especially Zin, whose airwork is wild. And I don't do anything backward. Don't ask me to do a back roll, don't ask me to flip over your back, I just can't. But for all my limitations, I've got solid groundwork, control, and charisma, or so they tell me.

"C'mon, Chen, do it!"

We expect a lot from Chen, since everybody knows that Asia is where the breaking is at right now. You can tell by the World Championship winners—they're all Asian. Sometimes we talk about saving up the money to take a trip over there, hitting the clubs where the breakers hang, learning from them. Chen says he's got relatives who could put us up in Shanghai.

When practice is through, we slide Zin's furniture back into place and the guys take off. I decide to stick around until Zin goes to work. I don't feel like going home.

Zin heads to the bathroom for a shower, and I raid the

fridge, grabbing pitas, hummus, pickles, cheese, and spreading them out on the table. Even when he's had dinner, he's always starving after practice.

Zin's one-bedroom is at the top of a five-story walk-up a few blocks from Evermore. He can afford to live by himself, thanks to drunk people who tip generously. The place has minimal furniture: a coffee table from IKEA, a worn leather couch, a kitchen table with mismatched chairs. It works out well because there's not much to move when we practice. For decoration, Zin put up movie posters—*Raging Bull, Scarface, Goodfellas.*

He comes out a few minutes later smelling like clean. He looks at the table. "Sweet." Then he starts to eat, fast and two-handed, like he's afraid you're going to take his food away.

"We'll get them, you'll see." He's talking about the Spin-heads, of course.

"Yeah, we will."

"Spinman'll want the chance to kick us down. Won't happen."

I rip a pita in half and scoop up some hummus. I hadn't realized how hungry I was.

He looks into my eyes. "How are you?"

"Fine."

"Good." He squeezes my hand, a natural thing for him.

Zin lives by his own rules, and he does it well. My dad would say that he marches to the beat of his own drummer. It's true.

He doesn't judge success by other people's standards. He doesn't judge, period.

Neither does he talk about his past. Not much, anyway. I know that his family came from Yemen about twelve years ago and settled in Queens. Zin realized fast that he didn't exactly have golden-boy potential. He knew practically no English, and what he picked up, he picked up on the street. By sixteen he'd dropped out of school and started working as a busboy. He moved out on his own when he started working at Evermore.

When people ask me if we're dating, I tell them we're just friends. But we aren't, not really. We're something more, and we both know it. Zin is magnet and I am metal. It's been that way from the start.

BEGUILING

The phone rings.

I hope it's a telemarketer. When it's the ghost, you know dinner's ruined.

Mom answers it, leaves the room with the phone. Dad and I are thinking, but not saying, *What now? What kind of trouble is he in, and how much money does he want?*

I don't take another bite of my food. If I eat when I'm tense, I get a stomachache. I can already feel the muscles in my gut tightening up.

Tonight is my dinner night, and I made enchiladas poblanos. It's slices of chicken in a wrap, smothered in guacamole and covered in cheese. I ordered something similar last week when I went out to eat with Zin and figured I could do it myself. My parents were impressed.

Dad continues to eat. I watch my food get cold.

Mom comes back a few minutes later. She always looks like

she has a cold when she's upset—nose red, eyes watery. "He's been laid off."

Amazing, but he's never been fired. Laid off every time.

Yeah, right.

It's amazing that he can still crush her hopes. It's amazing that she still has hope. Hope that he'll keep a job, hope that he'll clean up. Hope that he'll get help.

I hate seeing her upset. Hate it.

"How much does he want this time?" I ask.

Mom shakes her head. She doesn't like to talk about the amount of money flowing from their bank account.

"Why don't you just cut him off?" I ask.

"We don't want him on the street." Mom's answer never changes.

They don't want him homeless. They will give up every last cent so they at least know he has a roof over his head.

"For all we know, he could be homeless already," I say. "Was he calling collect?"

She nods. "He said he's staying at a rooming house. It's three hundred a month."

"He can get that money from the government."

"We'd prefer it come from us," Dad says. It's a moral thing with them. Although the ghost is an adult now, they still consider him their child, their responsibility, not the state's.

"But you know what he's using the money for."

"If we can't stop him from using, at least we can stop those dealers from coming after him," Mom explains, as if we haven't had this conversation a hundred times.

"You're enabling him. Maybe if he didn't have money, he'd stop." But I don't believe that. Still, I feel I should come up with a solution. Every problem has a solution, right?

The truth: I know he won't stop. I know he'll do anything to feed his habit. And I've heard what guys sometimes do to pay for drugs. And I don't want that. I can't even think of that.

I hate that they're giving him money. But I'm glad they are.

Two hours later my cell rings.

It's Zin.

"Training?" he asks.

"'Course." I'm breathing hard. I wipe the sweat off my forehead with a swipe of my palm.

"How about taking the night off?"

"What, you're gonna entertain me?"

"Sure. I'm not working tonight."

"Great. Let me shower. I'll be over soon." I pick up my boom box and head down the hall to my room. Mom and Dad have designated the extra bedroom as my workout/training room, which means I don't have to brave the dank, unfinished basement.

After a shower, I give my hair a quick upside down

blow-dry and let it hang loose around my shoulders. My outfit is my usual jeans and a purple velvet hoodie.

An hour later I buzz his apartment.

No answer. Maybe he's in the shower. I wait a few seconds, then try again. No answer.

I check my cell to see if he left a message. Nada.

"Nic!"

I look around, see nothing.

"Up here!"

I crane my neck. Zin is standing on the roof. "Are you coming up?"

"Are you gonna buzz me in or what?"

"Can't you climb? I did!" He laughs. "Fine! I'll buzz you in!"

Seconds later I hear the buzz, and I skip stairs up to the roof. Breaking's given me the kind of endurance that lets you do that type of thing without feeling like you're having a heart attack.

Speaking of heart attacks, Zin is standing in the doorway of the roof entrance, illuminated by the glow of a nearby streetlight. His black hair looks wet, as if he just showered. He's wearing a long-sleeved black tee and jeans, typical attire for him, even though it's February. I've told him more than once that he'll catch his death dressing like that, but he doesn't care. He says his Arab blood makes him immune to cold. I say that's the stupidest thing I've ever heard.

"Nic, you've come."

He's always saying things like that. It's as if me coming over is a special event or something.

He opens his arms and catches me in a hug. He has a way of hugging me like he means it.

"I'm glad you called. I needed to get out."

"Something wrong?"

"No more than usual."

"He called?"

"Yeah. Money, same old. It's nothing we haven't dealt with before."

"I know. Still."

I breathe deeply against his chest, like somehow I'm getting air from his lungs.

"I didn't want to see the show alone," he says.

"What show?"

"The universe's birthday."

"That's a new one."

"Actually, it's an old one. Come."

He leads me across the roof, climbs on top of a big block of concrete, probably a generator of some kind, and pulls me up. On top is a wool blanket.

"Now hold still."

He wraps me up, swaddling me like a baby. "If you're not warm, you won't have the patience to wait."

"I'm not the one who's gonna freeze, Zin. It's thirty degrees."

"I drank tea, don't worry."

I roll my eyes, then sit back. "So what are we looking for?"

"You'll see."

I look up at the stars, drinking in a breath of cold air, exhaling white mist. "You're a bartender, a dancer, a philosopher, and now an astronomer. Am I missing anything?"

"You're missing a lot of things." I can hear the smile in his voice.

"You know what, Zin? Sometimes I think you came to America just to entertain me."

"Sometimes I think so too."

We sit in silence. Just like Zin to know the exact moment of some spectacular event.

The blanket and his closeness keep me warm. I feel his hand touch mine.

"There."

I follow his finger, and then I see it, above Orion's Belt. A shower of fiery golden bursts.

"Wow. What was *that*?"

"A meteor shower. I call it the universe's birthday because it looks like fireworks in space."

"That's amazing." I turn to him. His face is a pale blur in the darkness, but I see the outline of lips smiling. "Thanks for showing me."

"Thank you, Nic. Aloneness is overrated."

"Yeah." But the truth is that if we weren't together tonight, he wouldn't have to be alone. There are any number of girls who'd love for him to call. Girls flock to Zin. Not only breaker groupies—and he has enough of those. Everyone. Even the waitresses at Evermore adore him.

But Zin and I have something in common; we don't like stillness, we don't like quiet. I have too many thoughts of a ghost. Zin's mind works a mile a minute, and if he isn't focused on something, he'll start thinking deep thoughts and eventually feel down. He says it's the curse of being philo-sophical.

"Do you ever wonder about the end of the world?" He throws the question into the darkness.

"Not a lot." But I want to keep him talking. "Do you think about it?"

"Only if I let myself. It's depressing. I don't like to think of what comes . . . at the end."

"It's not like we'll be around to see it."

Out of the corner of my eye, I see his head turn my way. "Maybe we will."

"You believe in reincarnation?"

"I'm not sure. I just know that everything must have an end. No matter how long we go around in circles, someday, sometime, it will all stop."

"What does Islam say?"

"It tells of a day of judgment—a day when God accepts the good people into paradise."

"Like Christianity, I guess. Heaven for the righteous."

He looks at me. "You believe in heaven?"

"Yeah. Don't you?"

"No."

"I thought you were Muslim."

"I was, a long time ago."

"So what happened?"

"Events in my life took me in another direction."

"Well, maybe life will take you back one day."

"I envy you, Nic. Faith is comforting."

I think of my parents. They need God. So do I. "You probably think people invented God to comfort themselves, right?"

"Maybe."

"You might be right. Then again, you might not be."

"If I'm wrong, I'm screwed. I doubt God would let me in."

"Come on, Zin. Don't say that. You're one of the kindest people I've ever met."

"And one of the most selfish."

"Well, I don't see it. We all have flaws. If there is a God, I'm sure he knows that."

"Yeah, but some of us have more than we deserve. And if there's any justice in this world, we'll have to pay for it."

"That's morbid."
"That's life."

Ghosts leave things behind.

Objects moved from where they used to be.

Coins scattered in weird places.

Cold and warm spots where they once passed.

Guilt.

My parents wonder if they could have done something differently. Something that would have changed the outcome.

Should they have been harder with him? Softer?

And me, I have guilt too. Guilt for all the things I said. Guilt for words like "I hate you" and "Admit it, you fucked up," and "Get it together."

Guilt for wishing he would go.

Guilt for him going.

EVER
DARE

It's just a fact that Thursday night means Hip-Hop 'n Bowl.

After Rambo gets off work at nine p.m., he goes home to shower and cologne himself, then picks us all up in his fly ride. Too bad Zin can't participate in the ritual—while we're cruising out to Long Island for a prebooked lane at ten o'clock, he's starting his shift at Evermore.

The music is blaring, and I'm squished in the backseat with Chen and Kim. She keeps giggling, so I'm guessing he's feeling her up underneath her jacket, but it's too dark to know for sure. I like Chen and Kim, apart and together. They're a happy couple, but they don't make you feel like a fifth wheel if you're hanging around with them.

It hits me how much my life has changed since that night at the club when I saw the Toprocks in action for the first time. In those days, I hung around with the same group of girls I'd met in eighth grade when my family moved here from Connecticut. I had nothing in common with those girls, and when I drifted away from them, no one was surprised.

It was nobody's fault. I was always looking for something different, something I couldn't put my finger on. I'm not a tomboy, but I think I was born to be friends with guys—they laugh, they don't backstab, they make dirty jokes, and they don't give a shit.

And then there's Kim. She transferred into our school in September from JFK High because our school offered more AP classes. She's the type of girl that Chen's got to work to hang on to—the type who knows her worth. She has short black hair with a swathe of blue in her bangs and several gorgeous tattoos. Kim is not a breaker and has no interest in becoming one. Her idea of dancing is limited to intricate hand movements that, the guys tease her, make her look like a mime.

The bowling lanes are already hopping when we claim our lane and glide on the shiny floors with our smooth-soled bowling shoes.

"No, you didn't!" I say. Rambo has made good on his promise to buy his own bowling shoes—ultrashiny black ones.

He does a moonwalk and spin.

It's time to bowl. The only difference between Hip-Hop 'n Bowl and regular bowling is that there's loud hip-hop music. We often burst into spontaneous dancing.

Halfway through the first game, Chen and Rambo are competing for first place, with Slide not far behind. I'm in fourth, and Kim is hardly on the scoreboard, probably because she has skinny arms and has trouble picking up the ball in the first place. She has nothing to prove on the bowling lanes, though, and neither do I. We let the guys battle it out while we chat and eat vinegar-soaked fries.

"Too bad Zin can never come out Thursday nights," I tell her. "I know he'd love this."

She smiles at me, and I know what she's thinking. Part of me wants to deny it, but another part is dying to let her in.

"I've gotta be honest with you, Nic. The sexual tension is killing me."

"Huh?"

"Between you and Zin. When are you going to do something about it?"

"I . . . well . . ." I wasn't expecting her to put it quite *that* way. I chew on my lip. "Don't tell the guys, okay? It could really mess things up."

"The guys know there's something going on—or *about to* go on. They're usually clueless, yeah, but they see the way you look at each other."

"You don't think it's just me?"

"No."

"Then why doesn't he do something about it?"

29

"Why don't you?"

"*Me?* He's the confident one."

"Maybe. Maybe not. You won't know unless you make a move."

I shake my head. "I'm not going to make a move. But I'll leave the door open for him to. I've got to be sure it's the real thing, otherwise we'll just mess up our friendship. And I don't want to be just another girl, you know?"

"I know, and I think you're wise. Never give a guy what he wants right away if you want him to respect you."

"Is that how you operated with Chen?"

"That's still how I operate with him." She grins. "My man's a firecracker, but I love him to bits."

The first time I saw Zin, he was dancing. I was one of dozens of people crowded around as he and the Toprocks tore up the floor at an under-twenty-one club called Trix.

The air over the dance floor was thick with dry ice, stinging my contacts. Zin burned through the fog like a high-powered flashlight, and I couldn't look away for a second.

When the show ended, the Toprocks went to the bar for hydration. Instinctively I followed, squeezing through a crush of people, claiming a place at the bar with my elbow.

"Nicole, you showed up!" It was Chen, who was in my bio class. He and Slide had been trying to convince people all over the school to come out that night to support the Toprocks in battle. I'd gotten a couple of friends to go with me, but they were chatting with some jocks from another school.

"You guys were amazing," I said.

"Thanks!" Slide pounded palms with me. "Glad you came."

They introduced me to a skinny little guy named Rambo. I imagined the name was a joke of some kind, so I didn't question it. Then Chen tapped the gorgeous Arab guy on the shoulder, and he turned my way. I was hoping for a smile from him, but he just stared at me like I was some oddity.

"Nicole, this is Zin, our leader," Chen said. "The man behind the Toprocks."

"Hey," I said.

"Hey." Zin frowned. "What's with your eyes?"

"Excuse me?" I reminded myself that he wasn't asking for the usual reason, since I was wearing my contacts. "Oh, dry ice irritates them."

"That's not what I mean. You're covering your eyes. Why?"

My mouth dropped open. No one had ever pegged my dark brown irises as contacts before. They were the most sensible, realistic-looking ones I could find.

Seeing my discomfort, he touched my hand. "It's cool. So, you liked the breaking, huh?"

"Uh, yeah. I've always wanted to learn."

That's when Zin showed me, for the first time, the smile that could light up a room.

◆ ◆ ◆

Friday night. Finally.

I've waited all week for this, to glide around in the stunning sanctuary vibrating with DJ Gabriel's rhythmic beats. I can't get over the beauty of this place.

"I missed you!" Viola, white blond and sleek, is changing in the back room where I go to drop off my bag. She has a slight British accent, which adds to her elegance.

I glance over my shoulder, just to make sure she's talking to me. "Thanks."

Her blue eyes sparkle. "Big tips tonight, I can feel it."

"I hope so. Last week was pretty good, for a first shift."

"You took to the job right away. You've been a waitress before."

"Yeah." At Denny's, I don't add.

"Well, Carlo was impressed. That's what's important."

"Did he say that?"

She shrugs a shoulder, bare in her blue sequined halter. "He doesn't have to. I've worked for him for a while. I can tell."

"Cool."

I didn't expect Viola to be so nice, I don't know why. Okay, I do know why: because she's beautiful. Irrefutably, magazine-cover-model-without-the-need-for-airbrushing beautiful.

Does anyone have the right to be so damned gorgeous *and*

sweet at the same time? It doesn't help that she and Zin are good friends.

"You should be out there by now, ladies." We turn to see Daniella, Carlo's younger sister, who occasionally pops in to give orders and act important—at least, that's how I see it. She has the classical Italian look you might find in a Renaissance painting, without the subtle Mona Lisa smile.

From what I hear, Daniella has it good. I've never heard of another person in their midtwenties being an art buyer, and one who buys for her own collection, at that. I suspect it's a Carlo-funded venture. Must be nice.

Viola and I head into the bar, stopping by the DJ booth to say hi to Gabriel, a handsome black guy with a shaved head. He doesn't have the personality you'd expect of a club DJ—he's focused, serious, not flirty. I don't know his story yet, but he intrigues me.

In fact, most of the staff intrigues me. I still can't believe how lucky I am that Carlo gave me this chance. It's not about the money, though the money is good. It's about being part of the staff at the coolest club ever. It's about the loud, throbbing music that wipes out all unhappy thoughts, leaving nothing to worry about except my next drink order.

After eleven the customers come in steadily. Mig and Richard like to keep them waiting out in the cold for a few minutes to build their anticipation. And a lineup outside always attracts business.

The other Toprocks show up just before midnight and hit the dance floor. We're all hoping for a battle tonight, but by one thirty it's clear that no other group, Spinheads or otherwise, is going to show up. I take my fifteen-minute break to dance with the guys.

After last call, the staff hits the dance floor. It was one of the first things Zin told me about Evermore: Carlo encourages his staff to end the night with dancing to blow off steam. Of course, I'm always down with that.

Once the front doors close and the last customer is gone, the party kicks up. This is the time of night when Mig is notorious for chugging down a few beers, ripping off his shirt, and going into a tirade of air guitar and head banging. It isn't the most pleasant sight (or smell) since he's been in his suit all night and he's sweaty, but as long as he doesn't grab me and swing me around like he's doing to some of the other waitresses, it's cool with me.

Viola drags Carlo onto the dance floor, and he dances for a minute or two before going back to his bar inspection. He isn't the type to let loose. Too bad—I bet he could move well if he'd learn to let go.

By the time the music shuts off, I have a full-on dance high. I should be tired—it's almost four a.m.—but I feel more alert and awake than I have all week. I can see that Zin's feeling the same way.

"My place?" he says. "Pizza?"

"Sure."

Zin puts on a jacket for once but lets it hang open. I dive into my parka, hat, and mitts and bend my head against the cold wind.

Zin knows these streets and the people who haunt them. He greets the homeless huddled in doorways, the strung-out drug addicts, the prostitutes. He always has a wad of dollars and change to give out, but only if they ask for it.

Sometimes I think he's kind, other times I think he's the neighborhood chump. When I pointed out that a raid on a crack house had uncovered thousands of dollars in dollar bills and quarters, Zin simply said, "Every dollar's a choice."

Chump or not, I like that he cares about these people. I pity them, but I'm repulsed, too—their vacant eyes, their smell, their hopelessness. All of it brings me back to the ghost.

Where is he right now?

"I'm thinking meat-lovers. What are you thinking?" Zin has a way of interrupting my thoughts just when they're sliding.

"Anything but anchovies."

"I can handle that."

Zin's place is warm and cozy, unlike my parents' house, where the furnace doesn't pump heat like it used to. But still, I'm never warm enough. Zin says it's because I don't have enough body fat—he should talk. I grab an afghan off the couch and drape it over my shoulders while he orders the pizza.

I settle on the couch. He sits beside me, drinking Coke, looking peaceful. "You know, it's great to have you at Evermore. I can hardly remember what it was like before you worked there."

"It was awesome—that's why I applied."

"Yeah, that's true." His head rolls back against the cushions. "I made a shitload off that bachelorette party. You usually don't get that kind of money in February. More people are getting married down south these days."

We're close on the couch, as always. Maybe it's a cultural thing that Zin has no personal space. I certainly have it, just not with him. Our thighs are touching. There's a vibe between us; I'm sure he feels it too.

He's studying my face, and I feel something rise inside him, like a question.

"God, I love you, Nic."

We both go still.

He gives an awkward laugh. "I scared you there. I didn't mean it . . . like that."

"You didn't scare me."

There's a tight silence. He laughs bigger now, but it's not his natural laugh. "We're not . . . that kind of thing." He reads my face. "Oh shit, Nic."

I look away.

"It would never work, you and me," he says softly.

I'm not buying this line from him. I've seen him go for plenty of girls without caring if it worked. Why not give us a shot? And if it doesn't work, so what? At least we tried.

But I'm not saying any of this. Because he knows this. He knows we're magnet and metal. It was bound to come out sometime.

"You're very special to me." His words are choppy. His accent always gets stronger when he's agitated.

Special? I want to gag. "I don't need pizza. I'm calling a cab." I get out my phone, but he stills my hand.

"You're not listening. Look at me."

I do. I look into his beautiful green eyes.

"I don't want to hook up, because I know it won't last. Why ruin this? It's almost perfect."

"You can't be faithful, is that it?"

"No. It's just that . . . I'm not the guy you'll want a few months from now when you're in college."

I frown. "You're worried I'll dump you because you're a bartender?"

"Something like that."

"Gimme a break, Zin. You don't need to make excuses. You're not feeling it, and that's fair. Just stop being so . . . lovey-dovey with me, okay?"

"I'm sorry, Nic. I never meant to lead you on." He looks so innocent, so sincere. It pisses me off.

"Oh, shut up. I buy a lot of things from you, but not insecurity. You're the cockiest bastard I know. So don't play this not-good-enough-for-me shit. It's not you."

His eyes drop to his soda can. "Me, I'm going to stay at Evermore for as long as it lasts. You, you're going to make something big of yourself. This breaker stuff is just a phase for you. You need this right now, but one day you'll outgrow this scene, and me."

"You're so patronizing, you know that? Have I done anything to make you think I don't take breaking seriously? What about my job—you think it isn't the best thing in my life right now? Well, it is. I'm not leaving Evermore anytime soon. In fact, I'm probably not even going to college next year."

His eyes flicker. "You're not serious."

"It's true. There's no money. My parents are in debt because of my brother. And I've decided I'm not taking a penny from them. I believe in a person paying for their own education anyway. I'm probably going to take the next year or two off and work as many hours as I can at Evermore. So there, I'm not going anywhere for a while. But that doesn't change anything, does it?"

I can't see his eyes, because he's hanging his head. His whole body is wired up with tension, the veins in his arms standing out like he's poised for a backflip.

This time, when I call for a cab, he doesn't stop me.

We go downstairs to wait for the cab. The cold wind whips

my face, but I can hardly feel it. I wasn't prepared for things to come crashing down with Zin. I wasn't prepared for this at all.

I could have stopped it, but I didn't. I wanted the truth about how he felt. And still, it doesn't feel real. I really thought he felt the same way.

The cab pulls up, and Zin puts his arms around me, those strong, wonderful arms, and squeezes me against him. "I'm sorry, Nic. I know you don't understand, but trust me. I'm doing the right thing for you."

His words have no meaning to me.

LONELINESS
UNBROKEN

Monday morning I fall into my seat, feeling like scattered pieces. Humpty. I don't know how to pick them up, much less how to put them back together. Dumpty.

Seeing him at work Saturday night tested my keep-it-together skills, but I pulled through. I had no choice but to find a way to handle this. My work, my friends, my dancing, they're all connected with Zin. I can't lose all of those things, I just can't.

I guess Zin and I were never friends, not on my side anyway. My friendship was tangled with my love for him.

I force myself to pay attention to my surroundings. Ms. Castleman is assigning group work, which I suppose means I should function. But then, I have Eli McCann in my group, who is all about taking the lead, even though the results will be less than stellar. Well, I'll let him.

Eli snaps up his pen and starts assigning tasks to me and Cass, the other girl in our group. We'll be doing a PowerPoint presentation on antioxidants. I already know what foods have them, because Dad's a health nut, but I passively watch Eli come up with a plan of action.

The bell rings. I go to my next class. My mind drifts in and out of focus. When Ms. Rankin questions me on the passage of Aristotle we're reading, I splay my hands because I don't have the answer she's looking for.

At lunch I do the bagged veggie thing with the guys, then we cross the street to Dunkin' Donuts for coffee. I ask for extra cream, since my stomach is already acid. My friends have no idea I'm sad because my dream of Zin has died.

When my watch says we have to go back, I can't do it. "I'm cutting this afternoon. Anyone else want to?"

Kim makes a face. "I would, but I have a quiz."

"I'm down with it," Chen says.

"Me too," Slide says. He's already on his cell with Rambo, who goes to Murrow High School in Midwood. "Yo, wanna come get us?"

Rambo is not the kind of guy to turn down the opportunity to ditch school, pick up his Toprocks, and cruise around Brooklyn. I feel slightly guilty at being the one to suggest we cut, since usually I'm trying to convince them to go to class. Today, though, I just can't stand the idea of sitting in a classroom another few hours.

Twenty minutes later we pile into Rambo's Nissan, which

smells like cologne, as usual. I pop into the backseat, feel the loud bass rattling the trunk. Chen slides in next to me.

Rambo weaves into traffic. "Let's see what Zin's up to." He tucks an earpiece in and dials. "Zin, what up?"

Damn it. If I'd known he was going to offer to go all the way to Manhattan to pick up Zin, I wouldn't be here. What's Zin going to think when he finds out that I suggested we cut the afternoon? Is he going to think this is some ploy to see him before practice tonight? Or will he think I'm too broken up to go to class? Neither is a good scenario.

Zin's on speakerphone. "What's happening, Bo?"

"We're all in the car looking for a destination. You up for it?"

"Can't, I got stuff to do."

"Aw, c'mon."

"*C'mon!*" Chen and Slide join in.

"Nah, really, I'm busy, but I'll see you tonight."

"What you busy with?" Chen asks. "Studying for your GED?"

"You got it, Bruce Lee."

I elbow Chen in the ribs. The one thing I can never get used to is how mercilessly these guys tease one another. I don't mind so much when they call Zin a terrorist, since he jokes about it himself, but the GED thing is a little much. We all know Zin didn't finish high school, and though he acts like he doesn't care, he can't be proud of it.

Damn it, I shouldn't be feeling sorry for him. He makes his own decisions.

I know that far too well.

That night at practice, I'm as ready as ever to hit the mat. As for Zin, he's quieter than usual. He looks nervous, like he's worried I'm going to get all emotional on him. But it won't happen. Friday night was bad enough. I don't get off on drama.

What do I have to dog him out for? Zin didn't do anything wrong, he just didn't return my feelings. Shitty for me, but not a crime.

So we practice, and critique Rambo's aerials, and I work on cranking my six steps up to eight. And we talk trash about the Spinheads and how their girl can't really dance, not like I can.

It's just too bad that I'm still attracted to Zin.

Pheromones suck.

I hoist myself into a handstand, wobble, then smack down onto my back.

"Ouch." Chen stands over me, laughing. "A little trouble concentrating?"

Tuesday night at the Y. Chen is here every night around nine, and sometimes I join him. The membership is cheap and there aren't many people around—none who care what we're up to. Just a few guys with barrel chests and skinny legs who like to watch themselves pump iron in the mirror. Guys who grunt so that everyone can hear how much weight they must be lifting. Guys who wouldn't notice me unless I wore tight exercise gear, which I never do.

I get up off the mat. "Guess I'm not myself tonight."

"Same as last night, huh?" He searches my eyes. "We all know something happened between you and Zin. You seemed upset yesterday, and then at practice we knew something was up. I didn't want to ask in front of the others. . . ."

I blink. So much for thinking the guys were clueless. I don't know what to say. I'm not sure what Zin told him.

"We figured he finally made a move on you. Poor bastard. It's obvious he's liked you for a long time. Go easy on the guy. He'll get over it. Slide was worried you'd get all freaked out and leave the group."

"I'd never do that—leave the group, I mean. I'm not freaked out."

"Good."

Wow, they really want me. I knew they liked me, admired my hard work. But the fact that they'd actually been worried I'd leave the group—it feels good.

"Spot me, I'm gonna do a double back." He bends his legs, getting into position.

"Wait, Chen. I should tell you, Zin and I . . . it didn't happen like that. He didn't do anything to make me uncomfortable."

He shrugs. "Hey, as long as everything's cool."

I spot him, though he doesn't need it. His airwork is always solid—his gymnastics training, no doubt. Chen is known for his precision, while Zin is known for the incredible height of his airwork. Chen, unlike Zin, is ambitious, and he's auditioned for several TV dance shows. He landed a top fifty spot in one of them last year.

Hearing the guys' take on the situation helps. Over the past few days I've wondered if the vibe between us was an illusion, a delusion. But if everyone else saw it so clearly, then it wasn't. I had reason to take the risk I did, to call him on it.

I still wonder why Zin didn't bother to take a chance. His reasons didn't feel real. *I'll be at Evermore for as long as it lasts.* Does he think I'm too snobby to date a bartender? It's dumb, and Zin isn't dumb.

Whatever. It doesn't change that I miss him, and that I hope we'll somehow find our way back to friendship through this.

"Any more auditions coming up?" I ask Chen.

"Dance America, but not till July. Rambo and Slide are gonna audition this time. You should too."

"I'll think about it." But I know I'm not at the professional level and never will be. I'm good, but not gifted, not like Chen or Zin. And I'm cool with that. "I'll definitely help you guys train."

We practice a few more moves, then go to the weight room.

I curl some hand weights while he does the leg press.

"How's it going at Evermore? Making mad money like Zin says?"

"Maybe not as much as Zin says, but it's better than Denny's."

"What about that Viola girl—is she single?"

"Hello, don't you have a girlfriend?"

"Not for me, for Rambo. He's always drooling over her."

"I'll find out for you, but it's a long shot. She's gotta be twenty-five. I somehow doubt she'll go for a guy in high school."

"Rambo thinks he'll charm her with his robotics."

We laugh.

"Kim and I got our six-month anniversary coming up."

"Do you have big plans?"

"Whatever she wants. She's got it all planned, I'm sure."

"Did I mention that you and Kim are an adorable couple?"

He scoffs. "Adorable? Damn, you women are determined to mess with my manhood, aren't you?"

I smile. "We try."

I get home around eleven fifteen, exhausted. The house is dark. My parents are always in bed by ten thirty. Pouring myself a bowl of cereal, I go up to my room and put some tunes on low. It always takes me a while to unwind before I can sleep.

I take out my camera phone, flip back to the only picture

I have of him. Zin never poses for pictures, says he isn't photogenic—a weird thing to say for a guy who doesn't fuss over his looks. Unfortunately, this picture, which I snapped at the bar without him knowing it, is distorted. His face is pale and ghostly, like an amateur photo editor superimposed him in after the picture was taken. And there is a glaring spot of light behind him, as if somebody else snapped a picture with a flash at the same time.

The irony is not lost on me: Zin won't let himself be captured in a picture, or in real life.

UNMERCIFUL DISASTER

I longed all week for the frenetic pulse of Evermore, and now it's here.

Viola and I catch up on the week. She's having boyfriend issues (note to self: Tell Chen to tell Rambo she's taken). Her current guy is upset because her ex still calls. Thing is, she's friends with her ex and doesn't want to cut him off. I sympathize with her, but the situation seems glamorous to me. I wonder what it would be like to have two guys vying for my attention.

Business trickles in slowly, and we're off to serve customers. Carlo doesn't like us to stand around too long, even if it's quiet. I can often feel his eyes.

I approach the bar to fill my first drink order. Zin's looking good in a way that makes me gnash my teeth, but I manage a friendly smile.

"Think there'll be a battle tonight?" I ask.

"You never know. I bet Spinman's afraid to come back. He knows they just got lucky last time."

After decorating the edges of the drinks with fruit slices, he loads my tray, and I serve them up to a new group of people on the velvet couches—a loud, seedy bunch that smells like weed and BO.

I stop dead.

It's the ghost.

A girl in his group is talking to me. "Gimme that Omega Cocktail thing. Did you get that?"

I didn't get that. He's going to spot me any second now.

The ghost looks up, double-takes. Then he looks away and keeps talking to his friends, like he doesn't know me.

"How are you, Josh?" I ask.

The group is buzzing.

"You know that girl, Cactus?" someone says.

He shakes his head. Then he gets up and heads for the bathroom like it's nothing, like *I* am the ghost.

I grab the back of his shirt.

"The fuck's your problem?" He pulls his T-shirt from my clenched fist.

"What are you doing here?"

"I should ask *you* that." He looks me up and down with cold blue eyes. "Playing grown-up, huh?"

"It's . . . good to see you."

50

But it isn't good to see him. It's terrifying. He looks like death. His skin is mottled with red bumps, his goatee is ratty, and his eyes look huge in his sunken face.

His lips curl. He's laughing.

He sticks his face in front of mine, giving me an eyeful. "You like seeing me, huh? That's not what you said last time."

"You don't have to live this way, Josh. We'll get you help."

"Yeah? If you want to help me, loan me fifty bucks."

"I can't . . . sorry."

He snorts. "See? You don't want to help me. You want me to follow your rules, live my life your way. Just like Mom and Dad."

"You've got a lot of nerve talking about Mom and Dad. They do everything they can for you."

"They kicked me out."

"You were using in their house! What did you expect?"

"You don't get it. You never did. Why don't you do your job and grab me a beer?"

I have to walk away. If I don't, I'm going to lose it. I turn, but he grabs my arm and yanks me back. I lose hold of my tray, martini glasses shattering on the floor.

Shouting and motion around me.

Carlo has him in a headlock. Josh is freaking out, shouting, writhing. Carlo sucker punches him and Josh drops to his knees, gasping.

The doormen drag him away. Josh's friends are shouting curses—they take them, too.

Carlo's arm is around me, holding me up.

"Are you okay? Do you want to tell me what happened?"

I can't. I can't speak. I can't stop crying.

Carlo takes me into the office, sits me down on the couch. He hands me a tissue. I pat my eyes, but the sobs won't stop. I can't believe this is happening. I'm going to be fired, I know it. He doesn't want a basket case on his staff.

Josh. The ghost. He'll never come back to us now. Never. He hates me.

Eventually I look up and realize that Carlo is still there, patient as ever.

"I know I'm fired."

His black eyes are soft. "You're not fired, Raven."

It's a term of endearment, and it makes me smile a little. "Thank you."

"Did you know him?"

Here it is. A chance to tell the humiliating truth.

"He's my brother."

He nods, wanting me to go on.

"I haven't seen him in months. He only ever calls my house to ask my parents for money. He's on meth and won't let anyone help him."

"I'm sorry." His eyes are steady.

Mine blur with fresh tears. "What happened—it's my fault. I keep thinking maybe there's some way to get through to him. But everything we've tried just makes him angrier."

"It sounds like you lost your brother a while ago. That guy out there, he wasn't your brother. He was a junkie. He's not the same person you knew. His soul is broken."

"But I still love him."

"You love the memory of him, Raven." He pulls me to his side. He doesn't even care if my tears mess up his suit.

After leaving me for a minute to check that everything is okay at the front, Carlo comes back to the office. We talk. An hour or two goes by, I don't know how long. I tell him things that nobody knows but Zin and my parents. I tell him about the hell when Josh was around, and the hell since he left.

At one point I see Zin hovering in the doorway. Carlo sends him away. Good. I don't want Zin right now. I don't want to need him anymore.

Eventually Carlo checks his watch. "I'd better get to the front. We're closing."

I can't believe it; we've been talking the entire night.

He offers his arm, helping me up. "Let me put you in a cab."

"But I can help clean—"

"Not tonight."

I walk out of the office with him, and I feel the staff watching me as we leave the bar. There's a cab out front, there are always a few, and Carlo opens the door for me and stuffs some bills into my hand. "Good night, Raven." Leaning forward, his chilled lips touch my forehead, and I sink back into the seat.

I am watching the ghost through a two-way mirror. He is wearing torn jeans and a T-shirt, scrunched where I grabbed it. His brown hair is mussed, like it hasn't been brushed or washed in days. He is sitting amid a group of people. It's his turn to speak.

"My name is Josh and I am an addict. I'm addicted to caffeine. To fast food. To my ex-girlfriend, who is kind of a slut. To playing with Ouija boards. To adult chat rooms. To Grand Theft Auto. To surfing the Internet for pictures of Scarlett Johansson, who is totally hot. To staying out all night. And maybe, just a little, to meth."

Everybody's looking at him, nodding sympathetically.

He turns to the mirror, looking straight through it. At me.

"Is that what you want to hear, Nic?" He grins.

The scene changes.

I'm at the morgue. I know it's a morgue because it's just like the one on CSI. *Cold, bare, blue. He's lying on a table, a sheet up to his neck.*

There's a figure in a black robe beside him.

"No!"

I hug my pillow, sadness clogging my throat. He's not dead, I remind myself.

Not yet, anyway.

FAINT
FOOTFALLS

Saturday night Slide comes up to me and shouts in my ear, "Look who showed up!"

I turn to see the Roccafella Poppers warming up on the dance floor.

My pulse speeds up. It means a battle.

Good. I'm in the mood for one.

The Roccafella Poppers—named after the Rockefeller Breakers, some of the best breakdancers of the eighties—are a group out of Queens. Their leader, twenty-eight-year-old Kazaam, is a veteran of the scene. Battling with them is a rare treat. I wonder how Zin lured them into showing up.

After getting the okay from Carlo, I hurry to the back to change, then join the guys on the dance floor. Their faces are serious. We're determined as hell to win this thing.

It's Slide who starts the battle, doing some aggressive popping in Kazaam's face. He ends it by flicking his finger at the popper's chest. An eager crowd forms around us.

Kazaam comes back with some toprocking, then lifts his legs into a bunch of L-kicks before dropping into a coffee grinder.

His choreography is impeccable, and the crowd cheers. It's up to Chen to counter him. He starts off in a headstand, rising into a handstand. Then, in a hot move, he flips out of the handstand and lands in splits.

The crowd roars. Chen jumps to his feet, curling his finger to bring on the rebuttal.

Dusk and Roccafella's newest member, G. Night, march into the middle of the floor with perfect synchronicity, busting out robotics. Then they go to the ground and do windmills—G. Night with a little less speed than the veteran, Dusk.

Zin and Chen are up next, putting the Poppers to shame with synchronized headspins. They've been working on this for weeks, and it's paying off big-time.

I hit the floor to do a worm, wriggling around like a spineless jellyfish. Zin drops into another worm, followed by Rambo. Zin counts "Three, two, one!" and we push ourselves to our feet and freeze in different poses. On the third count, we do some robotics. Then we freeze again.

The crowd wilds out. The Poppers come out with a few more moves, but the momentum is ours. We've won.

We pound palms with the Roccafella Poppers. They're good sports about it. It's not a real-life beef like with the Spinheads.

A crowd of groupies surrounds us, congratulating the guys, batting their eyelashes. Nobody says a word to me, of course. The girls just sneer at me as they try to figure out if I'm with one of the guys. I keep my distance to show them I'm not.

Zin and I don't have the luxury of staying on the floor long. I'm still grooving as I change, throw on another layer of deodorant, and go back to work.

When I'm waiting at the bar for Zin to fix drinks, Carlo materializes beside me.

"Nice work, Raven."

I notice the five o'clock shadow, the manly musk of his cologne, and the liquid black of his eyes. Have I noticed those things before?

"Thanks, Carlo."

Zin piles drinks onto my tray. I feel his eyes burning into me, like he's reading my thoughts, like he's warning me not to go there with Carlo.

I don't see why it would be any of his business. I smile at Carlo and walk away.

We.

Kicked.

Ass.

Satisfaction keeps me warm as I walk in the frigid cold after my shift. I needed to win tonight. I don't know why. It doesn't erase what happened last night with Josh. It doesn't lessen the ache for Zin.

But for those moments, the Toprocks tore up the floor. And it felt damned good.

The streets are quiet. It's just a five-minute walk to the subway, and I've walked this route often enough. The dejected faces huddling in doorways are familiar and benign. Still, I wish I had Zin with me. He made the cold less biting, the dark less scary.

I hear soft footsteps in the snow behind me. Throwing a glance over my shoulder, I see it's a scraggly guy. I pick up the pace. By the sound of it, he's doing the same.

Downright nervous now, I break into a jog. A scan of the area tells me I'm all alone. I reach into my pocket and take out my cell phone.

"'Scuse me, miss?" calls a voice behind me.

I turn around. He has come up close enough that I can smell him. His eyes are shifty and bloodshot.

Calm down. He's no different from Josh. He probably wants money.

"Could you give me a buck for a hot chocolate, please?"

I'm not in the habit of giving money to junkies, but I will this time, since I'm in a vulnerable position and I don't want to piss him off. Closing my hand around some change, I reach out to give it to him.

He steps closer, his hand outstretched. His other hand, I notice, is buried in the pocket of his coat.

My instincts scream that I'm in trouble.

I jump back, turn to run. But he launches himself at me, knocking me over. I hit the ground, my forehead smacking the sidewalk beneath the snow. I'm stunned for a couple of seconds, then adrenaline takes over. I struggle like a wildcat as he tries to pin me. All I can think is, *I'm not gonna let you rape me, you junkie scum!*

My elbow takes him in his ribs, winding him enough for me to roll onto my side. He comes back with a flash of metal aimed at my chest. It punctures my parka but skids off. *Holy shit, he's got a knife. He's trying to kill me.*

I barely have time to scrunch into the fetal position and put my arms in front of my head when the next stab comes. A hot, searing pain goes through my arm.

For a moment it's like time stops. I think of my parents, and how unfair it is that someone's trying to murder me when they've been through so much already.

With both hands I grab his wrist and use every bit of strength I have to throw his next stab off course. He pulls back, yanking out of my grip. And then, through the barrier of my arms, I see him lifted up in the air and thrown. A thud. Zin is standing over me, his eyes glowing amber. I blink. I might be shaking with adrenaline, I might be gushing blood, but his eyes . . . they don't look human.

"Nic." He's on his knees, putting pressure on my arm.

There's a puddle of blood in the snow. My blood.

"Where'd he go?"

In answer, Zin glances over his shoulder. The guy is lying twenty feet away. It looks like he slammed into a wall and now he's crumpled in a heap at the bottom. He's not moving. I don't understand. There's no way Zin, or anyone, could have thrown him that far.

Zin picks up my cell and hands it to me. "Call an ambulance. I have to go. You can't tell anyone I helped you or that I was here."

"Don't leave me!" The adrenaline is starting to desert me, and I'm worried that I'm going to pass out. "What if he gets up and comes after me?"

"He won't. He's out cold."

"But—"

"Look, you can't tell anyone I was here. If you do, I'm in big trouble."

"But you helped me!"

"I can still be charged."

I stare into his eyes. The irises are pulsating like a heartbeat.

"Zin, your eyes . . . something's wrong with them."

"Nothing's wrong." He looks away, dialing 911 on my phone. "Talk. Tell them you pushed him against the side of the building. Do *not* look at him, okay? You'll just scare yourself. He can't hurt you now."

"Okay."

The emergency dispatcher answers.

"I need an ambulance. I've—I've been stabbed. Corner of Canal Street and—"

Zin's leaving me. I see him get up, walk in the direction of the druggie. He places a hand on the guy's head, and a bolt of light shoots up through his arm, spreading through his body, dissolving. My jaw drops. Zin tilts his head back, takes a deep breath, then stalks off.

"Ma'am, are you there?"

The dispatcher is talking. I'm speechless.

FIERY EYES

I got lucky. That's how the doctor puts it. That's how the nurses put it. My arm got slashed, but all I need is ten stitches.

"It'll be a scar with a story," the doctor says. I don't respond. My mind is an hour ago.

My parents are there. I assure them I'm okay, it was no big deal.

The cops think there's more to the story.

"I pushed him into the building."

"You must be extremely strong, miss. His skull was smashed in."

I'm holding my hurting arm, trying to look innocent—which, I suppose, I am. "Well, I'm no wimp, especially when someone's attacking me."

"There's a dent in the brick where his head hit."

"The momentum came from both of us."

"Are you sure you've had no contact with this person before?"

"I'm sure. I've never seen him in the area."

"So you spend a lot of time in that neighborhood?"

"Not really. I just go to and from work."

"Did you have a friend with you? Maybe someone who might've known this guy?"

"No. I was alone."

The cops are nodding. They want to believe me. This case can be open-and-shut for them.

"You're working underage at a club. Do your parents know about that?"

"They don't like it, but they pick their battles, you know?"

They're nodding again. "You shouldn't be on the streets at that time of night."

"I know. It was a stupid mistake."

"You're very lucky it turned out the way it did."

Yes, I feel like I've won the lottery.

I am lying against my pillows, staring at my fuzzy TV. I had a sweet TV in my room once, in the days of prosperity. Then Josh stole it and sold it.

I replay last night over and over in my mind like it's a movie and I'm watching from a darkened theater. A girl encounters a junkie on the street. There's a struggle, a scream. And the last scene is played in slow motion: A beautiful young man with flashing eyes approaches the guy lying on the sidewalk and—

A knock on my bedroom door. Mom peeks in. "Zin is here. Do you feel up to having a visitor?"

"I asked him to come over."

"Okay, I'll send him up."

Zin walks in moments later, closing the door behind him. He looks paler than usual, and uncertain. "How are you feeling?"

"I'm okay. Tylenol Three helps." I look down at my arm, which is bandaged and in a sling. "It's not broken. The doctor thought I'd move it less if it was in a sling. So I don't bust the stitches."

He sits on the edge of my bed. "What happened with the police?"

"I told them he attacked me, there was a struggle, and I pushed him into a wall. They're gonna go with my story. They'd have to be pretty stupid to believe someone of my size could do that, but I don't think they care."

He looks relieved. "Thanks for keeping me out of it."

I don't say anything. I have so many questions inside me.

"I was watching you from a hiding place until the ambulance came. I didn't leave you. I don't expect you to believe me, but it's true."

"I believe you."

"Thanks. I bet last night's a blur for you. You'll be glad to forget it."

"I saw what you did to him."

He sighs. "I didn't mean to kill him. When I saw that guy on top of you, I went crazy. Adrenaline does that to you."

"That's not what I'm talking about. You touched his head. A light shot out of him."

His eyes sharpen. "What are you talking about?"

"I looked, Zin. You told me not to look, but I looked. I saw what you did."

"You went through a lot last night. I'm not surprised you thought you saw strange things. It's probably normal. I can't believe what happened myself."

"I know what I saw. Your eyes were . . . weird."

"You lost a lot of blood. It sounds like you were hallucinating." But his accent emerges behind his words.

"Please, Zin. Tell me what's going on."

Nothing is going on. I'm just stronger than I look. And when I saw him hurting you, I lost it."

"Are you on roids or something?"

"No."

"Then . . . ?"

His eyes are pleading. "Let it go, Nic."

"I can't. I saw you kill that guy."

"He deserved to die."

"I'm not going to argue with that. But I don't see why you can't tell me what's going on. Don't you trust me?"

His eyes meet mine, laser green. "I trust you."

"Then tell me."

He's silent for a long time, staring down at his hands.

"Zin—"

"I need to know that whatever I tell you, you're not going to tell anyone, no matter how . . . disturbing."

"I won't, Zin." *You know how I feel about you.*

"I'm immortal."

Silence.

He glances at me, as if I'm supposed to respond. I just stare at him. I don't know what I expected him to say that would explain last night, but it definitely wasn't this.

"I nearly died a long time ago. A man, a magician, brought me back from the point of death." He pauses, as if he's not sure what to say next. "I know it's weird."

"A magician . . . brought you back from the dead," I repeat, like hearing myself say it will make it sound less insane. My brain is rebelling. What he's saying can't be true. It's impossible. It's sci-fi. And yet there is no rational explanation for what I saw last night.

"So how old are you exactly?"

He gets up and walks to the window. "Depends if you're counting calendar years or the physical body. I've been around for a while, but I'm physically a twenty-year-old, with every-thing that means . . . If I'd been forty when it happened, it would have been easier."

My mind is spinning. He's telling me he's just another horny twenty-year-old—except that he's been around for an extra-long time.

A tremor goes through his left arm; his right hand moves lightning quick to still it.

"Zin? Are you okay?"

"I'm fine." But he adjusts his position so that he's leaning against the window frame.

I scramble out of bed. "You're not okay, are you?"

He won't look at me. "I have to go."

He's halfway across the room when I grab his arm. "Wait!"

Our eyes lock. His irises are amber. I jump back.

He lowers his eyes, and in a second he's out the door.

That evening the doorbell rings.

I look through the peephole. Flower delivery guy.

I open the door.

"Hi! I have a delivery for Nicole Burke."

"That's me." Wow. I sign for it and set it down on the coffee table, removing the plastic. It's a black-and-white bouquet, with black velvety flowers and white silky ones. I open the card.

My dear Raven. I was horrified to hear of your encounter last night. Zinadin promises me you are doing well. I am hoping for your speedy recovery. Yours, Carlo.

In my dream, I am a raven soaring through misty clouds. The skies are ashen; there is no heat from the sun behind them. Icy winds slice through my silken black hair. I draw my wings into my body for warmth. Then I start to fall.

I wake up with a start. It's 3:36 a.m., and the room is dark except for the white glow of the streetlamp across from our house. I lie there for a few minutes, deciphering shadows on the ceiling.

I can't take this anymore.

I dial my cell phone.

He answers on the second ring. "Hi, Nic." His voice is weak, even weaker than before.

"I'm worried about you. You looked terrible when you left."

"I'm sorry I scared you."

"You didn't scare me, not really. I was just caught off guard. You're going to be okay, right?"

"Yeah. It'll take a couple of days, but I'll be fine. I'm immortal, remember?"

"I remember." A memory flits across my brain of Zin

crossing a busy Manhattan street with no fear of getting hit. I always thought he was crazy.

Zin clears his throat. "So . . . I didn't scare you off? We can still be friends?"

"Of course. Nothing has to change. You're still you, right?"

"Yeah. I'm definitely still me."

"Then we're good."

I hear him sigh. "You don't know how glad I am to hear you say that. I've always wanted to tell you what I really am."

"*Who* you are, not what."

"Right. Thanks."

WEAK AND WEARY

When I wake up the next morning my arm is still aching, so I might as well milk it for all it's worth and take the day off school. Mom offers to stay home from work to take care of me, but I assure her I'm fine. I'm not sure that I'm fine, though. Physically, I'm recovering. Mentally, I'm not so sure.

On the phone last night, in the velvety darkness, Zin's voice was all the comfort I needed. Everything made dreamy sense. So what if he's immortal? He's still my guy, my crush, my BFF.

But in the light of day, this immortal stuff has stopped making sense. I don't know if it's that or the Tylenol 3, but my stomach is downright queasy.

I keep hoping he's going to call and tell me I've been punked. If only I could spot the hidden camera in my bedroom, it would be all right, and things would be normal again.

I spend the morning shuffling around the house in my

pajamas. I can't concentrate on TV, homework, books, MySpace. I end up spending an hour reading about immortality on the Internet and finding nothing useful except for a not-half-bad Norwegian rock band.

By noon, I'm beyond stir-crazy. Finally I text Zin:

WHAT U UP TO?

NOTHIN STILL NOT WELL ☹ HOWS UR ARM?

OK HOW ABT I STOP IN?

U CAN BUT MY EYES ARE STILL WEIRD.

MY EYE IS WEIRD TOO LOL IM COMIN OVER C U.

C U.

I take the subway across the Manhattan Bridge. A guy dressed old school comes in with his little kid in tow. He puts down his boom box right in front of me, and they put on a show. Daddy's not a bad breaker. Son messes up a flip and hits his head on the floor, but jumps up and continues the routine without a hiccup.

I give Daddy a *Your kid should be in school* look and

shake my head when the kid comes around for money.

Getting off the subway, I head for Zin's, eager but nervous. Will he look better or worse than yesterday?

He buzzes me in. When I walk up the five floors, I find his door slightly open. He's on the couch, huddled in a blanket. It's a sunless day and he hasn't put on any lights.

"Come in. Help yourself to a drink if you like."

I shut the door behind me. Usually I lock it—it's that kind of neighborhood—but this time I don't, just in case.

"Whatever's out there is more dangerous to you than I am," he says.

He's got a point. I lock the door and join him on the couch. He looks very boyish with the blanket around him.

"You're worse today, aren't you?"

He gives me a reassuring smile. In his eyes I see a flicker of amber, but it's gone before I blink. "It always gets worse before it gets better."

"This has something to do with what happened the other night, doesn't it?"

"Something like that. It's complicated. My body will recover fast, though."

"A benefit to being . . ."

"Yeah."

"Can I make you some tea?"

"Sure."

I put the kettle on, find some loose Darjeeling in a cupboard, and pour it into a tea ball. Zin only drinks loose tea. I wonder if tea bags had been invented when he was growing up.

"Have you eaten?" I ask.

"I'm okay, thanks."

I wait in the kitchen for the kettle to boil. Then I bring the tea on a tray with some digestives.

He accepts the tea, taking a long drink. I blow on my cup a few times before taking a sip.

"Shit, I forgot honey. Want some honey?"

"I'm fine. Relax, Nic. You seem kinda keyed up. Not that I—" A tremor passes between his shoulders. "Not that I blame you."

"I've got to be honest, Zin. . . . I can't forget what you did to that guy. The light that came out of him. I want to know what you did to him."

"He was dying. His life force was going to leave his body. I just helped it along. You believe in the soul, don't you, Nic?"

"I do." I pinch my skin. "This is just a costume."

"I love that about you. You're so sure of your beliefs."

"I am?"

"Seems to me you are."

"You said some things that night on the roof. Things that are starting to make sense."

"That'll be a first."

"You talked about everything coming to an end."

"You know I get philosophical sometimes. It doesn't mean anything."

"If you're immortal, I guess you give some thought to things like the end of time."

"The magician who made me this way . . . he said there's no end to forever, and I am forever."

"How do you feel about that?"

He smiles. "I've got myself a mortal shrink, huh? Look, I don't think anyone can handle the concept of forever. Everything I've ever known has had a beginning and an end. The only thing that hasn't ended is my life."

"You said, that time, that you felt selfish, like you'd taken more than you deserve. And if there was a God, you'd have to pay."

"I don't believe in God, but I'm not saying there isn't karma. When you've lived as long as I have, you see that people get what's coming to them. That's the reason I sometimes worry about—" He hunches forward, a full-bodied tremor going through him. When it's over, he hangs his head. "I don't play by the rules, Nic. I wonder if the universe will notice."

"Sounds like you believe in a higher power."

"It doesn't matter what I believe. All that matters is what is."

"The magician who changed you—how did he do it?"

"I don't know the spell, and I'd never want to know."

"Why not?"

"I'd be tempted to use it. And a world full of immortals isn't practical."

"Does anyone else know about you?"

"This isn't something you tell anyone, not even a best friend. You can imagine what would happen if word got out. I only told you because of what you saw."

"I won't tell anyone. Ever."

"I know."

"Are there others like you?"

"I'm sure—" He steels himself against a tremor, then leans his head back against the couch. "There probably are. Only makes sense."

"Well, have you thought of finding them?"

"Should I put an ad in the paper?" He shakes his head. "Look, I'm sorry. I'm just not myself today."

"I'm sorry for asking so many questions. Maybe I shouldn't have come over. You probably just want to rest and get better."

He raises a shaky hand and touches the side of my face. "You're soothing. Don't leave. Let's just be."

"Okay." I'm not sure how I'm supposed to just "be," but I figure it means being quiet for a while. I'm good with that.

I look over at him, the pale face, the beautiful eyes that flash with fire. And I know that whoever he is, I still love him.

Magnet and metal, Zin and me. That'll never change.

◆　◆　◆

Tuesday at lunch. There are a dozen people crowded around me making various types of wow noises. It feels like I am describing an awesomingly bad date instead of the night I was almost murdered.

It's been this way all morning. When Mom called in my absence yesterday, she gave the attendance office the whole story. They gave the principal the story, who gave the staff the story, who decided I was a hero. I'm a school celeb now.

I keep thinking that if I'd died, they wouldn't be celebrating how strong I was that night. They'd be saying it was such a shame.

I was so close to being a shame.

But I can't think of my own mortality without thinking of Zin's lack of it. Maybe I should ask him to track down that magician and hook me up. Then I wouldn't have to worry about walking alone at night ever again.

"Sorry, guys, I've gotta get to class," I say. "Press conference is over."

"Wait! How does it feel to kill someone?"

The question jumps out at me from the crowd, care of a gawking freshman.

"I didn't *kill* him. I just pushed him and he hit his head. But I'm not sorry he's dead."

Everybody goes quiet. I walk away before anyone can stop

me. Did I just blurt that out? Damn it. I'm surprised by my words, by the truth in them. I'm glad the guy is dead so he can't hurt me or anybody else.

I just wish I could've saved myself. I had enough rage to rip that guy apart, but he was stronger than me. I'd do anything to have had Zin's strength for those moments.

"Nic!" Chen jogs up beside me. "Next time people swarm you like that, give me the word and I'll take 'em down."

"Thanks. I handled them. They probably think I'm a psychotic nut job, but I handled them."

"That's not what they're thinking—they're thinking you're a badass bitch. And I gotta admit, the whole thing blows my brain. I didn't know you were *that* strong. Are you sure you're not using protein shakes like I told you?"

I laugh. "Obviously *I* don't need them."

"Ohhh, what are you trying to say?" He grins. "You think you can battle me?"

"I could polish the floor with your ass." I look down at my arm. "Actually, I don't think I'll be battling for a while."

"Then neither will we. The Toprocks don't battle without one of their members."

"Thanks, but I don't want to hold you guys back. The Spinheads could come back anytime."

"They'll just have to wait. I'm not saying we won't practice, but we won't battle. Zin canceled practices this week anyway. Says he came down with something nasty."

"I heard."

"Anyway, I'll still be at the Y most nights if you feel like working out. I'd hate for your superhuman muscles to atrophy."

"It would be a shame, wouldn't it?" Something inside me stills. *I was so close to being a shame.*

"You okay, Nic?"

I nod.

He puts an arm around me. "I know this must've shook you up. There's nothing wrong with that." He winks. "At least you had some help that night, huh?"

I stare at him. "What do you mean? There was no one else there."

He smiles, then glances upward. "Maybe you got some help from upstairs. Don't tell me you haven't thought about it."

"Actually, I haven't."

SAD SOUL SMILING

It's my fault that Josh doesn't call the next week to arrange the wire transfer.

It's because of what happened at Evermore.

My parents are worried. I hear Mom telling Dad she wants to investigate different rooming houses. She needs to get a glimpse of him to know he's okay.

"What, you plan to go around to every rooming house in Brooklyn?" Dad says. "We don't even know if he's in Brooklyn."

"I can make some calls at least."

I'm standing outside the den. Their discussion goes in circles. It's the same discussion that went on this morning, last night, and all the days before. What to do about Josh. Where to look for him.

They're scared. Sometimes I wish they could just cut the umbilical cord and be done with it, but it doesn't work that way when you love someone.

I have to do something. I have to tell them the truth, or something else.

I walk into the den where they're sitting with the TV muted. "Don't bother, Mom. He called earlier today to say he didn't need the money anymore."

Mom's eyes light up. "Has he got a job?"

"I don't know. He didn't say."

"Did he say where he's staying?" Dad asks.

"No. You know he doesn't talk to me."

Behind his reading glasses, Dad is frowning. He wants to believe me, but I don't think he does. Josh has never changed his mind about wanting money before.

Dad just nods. He'll accept what I'm saying, whether he believes it or not.

I've discovered that full disclosure isn't always the best way to go. Sometimes you have to lie to protect the ones you love.

"Still no word from Josh?" Zin asks as we take a step forward in the ticket line.

"No."

"Shit."

"That sums it up."

I'm not a fan of outdoor movie lineups. Not when it's freezing out and my arm is sore and my mind is haunted by a ghost. Thank God for Zin. He can keep my mind occupied.

I only wish he'd share his body heat. He must have a lot to spare, standing there with his coat open.

Zin steps up to the cashier and pays for both tickets. As we walk into the theater, I ask, "What was that for?"

"I thought it was a nice thing to do."

"It is. Thanks. But don't go thinking this is a date, because I've moved on. Way on."

He glances my way, and we start laughing. I'm glad we can still joke around.

We grab seats in the middle of a row halfway to the back. The lights dim as the trailers begin. After each one, we give a thumbs-up or a thumbs-down. The only film that we agree has a chance of being decent is the raunchy Spanish one about a love triangle. I'll overlook the subtitles if it's juicy.

We're barely twenty minutes into the film when I realize it's a dead bore. I swear I've seen the same story line a thousand times with minor variations. It strikes me how ridiculous it is— I'm sitting here next to the most fascinating person I've ever met, and I'm wasting my time with this crap.

I want to know more about Zin, about his past. But lately he's been talking about anything but that, as if he hopes that if we don't talk about it, I might forget everything he's revealed. Fat chance of that.

I haven't pushed him, though. His health had me worried for a couple of days, but he's his old self again. He looks cuter and healthier than ever, like he's been re-energized at some celebrity spa. I glance at him, his profile etched in darkness. Still beautiful.

Sometime during the movie he shakes my shoulder.

I look up. "Wha'?"

"You were sleeping," he whispers.

Uh-oh. I don't need to ask if I was making noise. I've always mumbled in my sleep, ever since I was a kid. Which is why I mostly avoided sleepovers. Who knows what secrets I might give away?

Zin pats my arm. "Nothing incriminating. This movie sucks. Wanna go?"

I nod sleepily.

As we step out of the movie theater onto the street, the shock of cold air wakes me up. My body contracts under my coat for warmth. I'm not tired anymore, and I'm in no mood to call it a night.

I turn to Zin. "Your place for some food?"

"Sounds good."

We go into a deli for groceries. I grab a basket, which he takes from me. "Easy on your arm."

"It's feeling much better. I wish I could go back to work this weekend. It's going to be so boring at home."

"Wait till you get the stitches out. Don't worry, Carlo understands."

"He sent me the most amazing flowers."

"Did he?" He plunks a can of red beans into the basket. "How charming."

As Zin stir-fries chicken, I lean against the counter, watching him.

"I want to know more," I say.

"About what?"

"About you."

He sighs. "I'm sorry I lied to you about my past."

"It's okay. The truth wasn't exactly an option."

"What would you like to know?"

"Everything you're willing to tell me. Tell me about your childhood."

"I grew up in Yemen in the 1790s." He pours a dollop of hoisin sauce into the stir-fry, tastes it. "Childhood wasn't supposed to be fun. I don't think we even had a word for childhood. My dad died when I was six. My mother tried her best to make sure there was food. Lot of the time, there wasn't."

"God."

"Yeah. I begged for food in the market square. So did a bunch of other kids. I learned to flip and tumble to set myself apart. It worked."

"Must've felt good."

"Damn right. That was just the beginning. My routines

got better and better. People started going out of their way to see me perform. Eventually I got recruited for a circus."

"You were lucky."

"Luckier than the others, yeah. But circus life was grueling. It's a business like any other, and we were the product. We had to perform several shows a day. But they fed me, and I earned money for my family, so it was worth it. This is ready."

He brings the pan over to the table and pours its contents onto two plates. He dives in with his usual fervor.

After a few minutes of eating, I ask, "So what happened next, after the circus?"

"I got sick. Tuberculosis. Your lungs fill up. . . . I'd never want to go through that again." He uses some pita to soak up the extra sauce on his plate, then rolls it up and puts it in his mouth.

"How did you meet the magician?"

He finishes chewing before answering. "I didn't meet him until weeks after he changed me."

"You must've been so relieved to wake up and be healthy again."

"I was more confused than relieved. I'd been unconscious for days. By that time I wasn't experiencing any pain. It was . . . soft darkness."

"Was it scary, the darkness?"

"It was peaceful. There was no thought."

"So you didn't see a light or anything?"

He smiles. "Oh, right. You're a believer. No, I didn't see a light. When I woke up, I was disoriented. My family was crying with happiness. They told me I'd fought my way back from death. I didn't know anything about the magician until he came back a few weeks later."

"Did he tell you what it meant—that he'd made you immortal?"

"Yeah. He told me I wasn't going to age and that after a while, people would take notice. He told me I couldn't lead a normal life. I couldn't get married or conceive children. That was a huge blow. Back then, that's what people did. That's what being a man was. You had a wife and kids and you took care of them."

"That must've been awful."

"It was."

"Did you have a girlfriend?"

"Yeah." He picks up another forkful, scarfs it down.

I feel a stab of jealousy. I shouldn't ask more. I don't want to know.

But I can't help it. "You must've loved her."

"Yeah, well, there was nothing I could do. I couldn't marry her knowing that I wouldn't grow old with her and there wouldn't be children."

"Don't you think she would've married you anyway?" *I would have.*

"It doesn't matter. I didn't give her the chance." He puts his fork down, staring at his plate. "I left town for a while, but eventually I came back. I had forever to explore the world, but my family was only going to be around once. They were struggling, so I went back to the circus, brought home money. After a few years people began to notice that I wasn't aging. Some thought I was blessed by God. Others, like my mother, thought I was cursed. By letting the magician change me, she worried she'd made a deal with the devil; she thought it was all her fault for not being able to let go. I told her I didn't see it that way, but I had some bitterness of my own. Gradually I accepted the situation. Time works on you that way. I knew I was lucky to be alive. It was easier once I left the village after my family was gone."

"But you never felt like your mother had made a deal with the devil, did you?"

He shrugs. "What difference would it have made if I did?"

DEMON DREAMING

I'm the one who knows his secret.

I'm the one with a pass into his private world.

The door that was always closed is opening, and I am consumed. I don't know if a full minute goes by that I don't think of him, that I don't replay how it felt to have his hand brush mine, his eyes look my way.

And yet he's hiding, still. He talks as if my feelings for him are in the past, as if they couldn't possibly be relevant now that I know the truth about him. But I don't have that kind of power over how I feel. And if he doesn't know that, he's blind.

I spend my days in a haze of wonder, almost as if I've been given the ability to see the world as Zin sees it. What would it be like to be immortal? To have no fear of age, disease, or death? To walk the earth in search of every experience you've dreamed of? To never run out of time?

Zin hasn't lost his sense of the miraculous. He's fascinated by the stars, which he must have studied for lifetimes. And he's fascinated by the human body, and the way it can move. And I am fascinated by his body more than any other, and what it can do on the dance floor, and what I dream it can do to me.

We talk on the phone every night. He calls me from home or from work when he's on break. I close my eyes and listen to his stories of times past. Even the most mundane details fascinate me. I want to know how people lived, what they believed in.

"Has it been lonely for you?" I ask. It's so late that I've turned my alarm clock to face the wall so I won't have to be reminded. All I want is to be here with Zin, holding this connection. I can hear the steady flow of his breath on the other end of the line.

"Yeah. I've met so many people, and they don't really know me. I can't tell them who I am, or what I've lived. Even if I could, I probably wouldn't want to. It's not often I've met a person I really want to know better. But I knew I wanted to know you the moment I set eyes on you."

"You made an impression on me, too."

"Good. You haven't cut me loose yet, and I've given you plenty of reason to."

"No, you haven't."

"I'm glad you see it that way. I've tried to be truthful with you, but as you know, there are some situations where it's not an option."

"Of course. Some situations make you have to lie."

"Like with your brother."

I wish he hadn't reminded me, but it's true. I was never a liar before he became an addict. But I don't feel it's my duty to let everyone know what's happened to him. Some things are best kept quiet.

"I'm glad you know about me, Nic. I shouldn't be, but I am."

"No one wants to be alone with a secret."

"No one wants to be alone, period."

My arm heals with what Zin calls "mortal sluggishness," and I'm back to work in two weeks. The first shift is a little rocky because my arm seems to have forgotten how to balance a tray, and I have a couple of near spills. Thankfully, by the second shift I've hit my stride again.

The Toprocks won't be showing up tonight. Since we're not battling again yet, there's no need for them to stop in, and apparently Slide and Rambo are taking out some college girls they met at a bar yesterday. I really hope the girls don't just let the guys buy them drinks, then ditch them. Slide and Rambo are too innocent in that area.

I don't have much energy to dance anyway, since my body's getting back into the swing of things after vegging out for so long. In fact, I'm feeling overheated, so I grab my coat and go outside to get some air. Mig says hey and Richard gives me a formal nod of his blond head. Mig steps back from the lineup.

"I don't know if we officially welcomed you back. It's good to see you in one piece."

Which could be a tasteless thing to say, considering I could've been cut into pieces, but Mig means well.

"How are things going out here?" I can see the lineup is almost a block long.

"Gets busier every week. Good for business, but once we reach capacity, we have to keep people out. No matter how nice their clothes are." He laughs at himself. "Unfortunately, we're getting more and more characters who think they're entitled to get in, and they're getting aggressive about it. A couple of the gangs want this to be their new hangout. Some cat had the balls to try to get past us with a gun last week."

"That's scary. I'm glad you caught him."

"Me too. For the record, we're sorry we let your brother and his friends in. We figured they were harmless. Obviously we didn't know the connection."

"You couldn't have known. No worries."

Mig steps up as a guy in a bomber jacket tries to slip past Richard. They each grab an arm and fling him to the curb. The guy curses them out, to which Richard politely responds, "If you have a grievance, send a letter of complaint to our manager."

I head back inside, throwing my coat behind the bar.

"Fun out there, isn't it?" Zin says.

"That's one way of putting it."

"Don't worry. They're highly skilled, those guys."

"Shouldn't you be doing a job like that?"

"I have, and will again. But every few years, I go for something cushy."

"I've never asked you about all the jobs you've had, have I?"

"No, you haven't."

I'm about to try to get more out of him, but then I feel Carlo's eyes on me, and without saying another word, I go back to work. There are so many needy drinkers that it looks like Viola, and part-timers Jen and Amy, are being run off their feet.

I ride the wave, serving drinks and collecting tips left and right. At some point I have to slip away to the bathroom. Carlo, thankfully, trusts us to go to the bathroom whenever we want, unlike Janice, my boss at Denny's, who practically expected us to schedule a week in advance.

All of the stall doors are closed, but they naturally settle that way, so I have to bend down to see which ones are occupied. Someone is sitting on the floor of the far stall.

"You okay in there?"

No answer.

I push the door open. There's a girl slumped on the floor. I shake her shoulder, but she doesn't respond.

The girl's purse is open. I spot a scrap of tinfoil and don't need to see more.

I run out of the bathroom, find Carlo. "There's a girl in the bathroom—she's unconscious."

His brows come together. "Get Viola. She knows CPR."

"Should I call 911?"

His cell phone is already out. "I'll do it."

I find Viola with a tray full of drinks. "Some girl passed out in the bathroom. Carlo needs your help."

Her eyes widen, and she thrusts the tray into my arms and takes off. I put her tray down and follow her back there.

Carlo is kneeling beside the girl. "Nicole, stand outside and keep people from coming in. Tell them the bathroom has flooded."

I do what he says, standing in front of the door and turning girls away. But I keep feeling that I should be doing more, like warning Mig and Richard to make room for the EMTs, or helping Carlo and Viola to revive her. I tell myself to stay put and not second-guess Carlo's instructions.

That girl, that poor girl, could be dying. It could so easily have been Josh. He could be lying on a bathroom floor right now, his life slipping away.

I press my ear to the door but hear nothing. I open it slightly. Carlo and Viola are bent over the girl. Carlo's fingers are pressed against her neck as if he's checking her pulse. "It's time."

Viola places her hands on the girl's head. A light shoots up through her arms, making Viola's chest thrust out. The light spreads through her and dissolves. She jerks her head back and takes a deep breath. "Yes. I have her."

"Is she struggling?" Carlo asks.

"She doesn't understand what's happening yet." She looks at Carlo, her eyes gleaming yellow.

My hand jerks, and I release the door.

Oh my God. That light Viola took from her . . . what was it? Was it her soul?

"Where is she?" an EMT shouts, two firefighters behind him.

I point to the bathroom door.

They run in. Moments later I can hear them using a defibrillator. There's a crowd of people around now, and I'm being pressed against the wall as a group of girls try to get a view inside the bathroom.

It's too late. They won't be able to save her.

Viola took her soul.

That means . . . Zin took my attacker's soul.

A wave of nausea rolls over me. I hurry out an emergency exit and throw up behind the garbage cans. *This is just a bad dream. It's impossible to take another person's soul. I must have seen it wrong.*

I hug myself against the cold, trying to get a grip on myself, trying to make sense of it. But I can't. Because I know what I saw, and it's sickening.

The door swings open. Zin is there. "Nic, you're gonna

freeze! Come in." He waves me in, but I don't move.

He walks toward me. "I'm sorry you were the one to find her. It's horrible. A waste of a life. Come, we're closing up. Let's get you warm."

"I'm fine." I take a step back. I don't want him to touch me.

He frowns. "I can't leave you out here. You're shaking. You're gonna catch your death."

I'm not sure if he's threatening me or comforting me, but my stomach is roiling, and I'm pitted under my thin shirt. "I need a few minutes alone."

"Okay, but let me get your jacket." He catches my gaze, and his eyes narrow. "You're afraid of me. Why?"

I say nothing. If I speak, I might scream.

"Look at me."

I look at him, and his mouth opens in a soft gasp. "You saw."

I take another step back, but he comes closer. "I'm so sorry, Nic. I wish you hadn't seen that." He grasps my arms. "We've got to talk."

"Let go of me! Let go!"

He releases me.

I run.

And run.

Until fatigue and cold make me stop. I walk the dark streets in search of a cab. I'm not afraid of another junkie attack. I'm more afraid of what I left behind at Evermore.

I find a cab. It drops me home, which is dark now except for the orange glow of the porch light.

In my room I turn on every light, triple-check that my window is locked, close the blinds, and get into bed, piling the covers on top of me. It's 4:39 a.m. There is no question of sleeping. Not now, maybe never again.

I tell myself if I can just last through the night, I'll be okay. Just a couple of hours before dawn. Maybe three hours before my parents will be up. Surely they wouldn't come after me with my parents around.

Unless they want all of our souls.

I keep thinking of that poor girl in the bathroom. Of Zin bending over the junkie, stealing the light from him. Zin told me he was helping the guy's soul "move along," not that he was taking it *into* himself. I can't believe he lied to me.

What kind of a person takes the soul of another? It's inhuman, inhumane. I should have known by the flickering glow in his eyes that he was evil.

I remind myself that if Zin wanted to hurt me, he's had plenty of chance. Just because he can take someone's soul doesn't mean he'd want mine. We're BFFs, for God's sake. That could mean something to him.

But what about Carlo and Viola? They have no loyalty to me. Zin must have told them what I saw. They could be on their way here right now. How can I defend myself against immortals who can't be killed?

A knock on my window.

Please, let it be in my mind. Maybe it's just the creaking of the house.

Another knock, strong enough to shake the blinds.

I want to dive under the covers, but I don't move. If something's going to attack me, I want to see it coming.

I am not going to the window. I don't want to know who's out there. Even if it's Zin with pleading eyes, there is no way I am going to let him in.

Another knock. It's a polite knock, not a pounding; whoever it is obviously doesn't want to wake up my parents. Still, I won't be lured into going to the window. He—or they—can knock all night if they want. I'm not moving.

I brace for another knock, but it doesn't come. Seconds pass. Minutes pass. Nothing.

Whoever is out there is probably gone, or they want me to think they're gone. It doesn't matter. I'm not going to the window to check that it's clear. I am going to sit here until the sun comes up.

And that is what I do.

The sun rises at 7:04 a.m. My eyes are heavy, but I'm home free. I've lasted the night without being killed. Still, I wait until I hear my parents moving around before daring to get out of bed.

I pull open the blinds to find my cell phone and jacket propped against the windowsill. Opening the window, I feel a gust of frigid air as I bring them in.

My cell is blinking.

One new message.

The sound of Zin's voice makes me shiver. "Nic, I'm sorry you had to witness that. I can't imagine what you must be thinking. Do you remember when we were on the phone and we agreed that there are some situations that make you a liar, even if you don't want to be? Well—"

I can't listen to any more. I delete the message. He sounds so benign, so same-old-Zin, with that husky voice that makes me dreamy and heartachy. I can't afford to let him reel me in. My life is at stake here. My soul is at stake.

The cell phone buzzes in my hand.

Zin's number comes up. For a second my thumb hovers over the talk button, but then I flick the phone shut.

I already know too much. I don't want to know more.

Being immortal is one thing. Being part of a group of people who steal souls is something else entirely.

GENTLE RAPPING

If Zin cares about me even a little, he'll leave me alone. He'll let everything I've seen dissolve into a nightmare that will fade over time. One day I'll question if it ever happened.

But he keeps calling me. I turn off my phone. He calls my parents' line; I tell them I won't answer it because Zin and I got into a fight. My dad has the nerve to look glad. He was never Zin's number one fan.

By early afternoon I'm barely functional, so I lie down on the couch for a nap.

I am in a blue bedroom I don't recognize.

Zin is hovering over me.

"Nic," he whispers. "You're ready, aren't you?"

"For what?"

"Shh . . ." His lips curve in a smile, as if he knows a secret. "Just trust me." His face descends to mine.

It occurs to me that I should stop him from kissing me, but I can't remember why. Maybe I don't want to remember. I want to feel his kiss so badly.

Closing my eyes, I wait for the touch of his lips.

But it doesn't come. I open my eyes to find him gone. Glancing around, I realize that I'm not in the blue bedroom, but a mortuary.

I try to get up, but I'm paralyzed.

Oh my God. He's here.

Carlo is standing over me in a black hooded robe, a dangerous warmth in his eyes.

"I've been waiting for you, Raven. It is time." His black eyes turn molten gold.

Let me go! But no words come out. I can't speak. Can't move.

He places his hands on my head, and I feel my soul lurch. An excruciating pain goes through my chest.

"Are you okay, honey?"

I open my eyes. Mom is kneeling beside me.

"Uh . . . yeah."

She searches my eyes. "Are you sure?"

I sit up. "I'm fine. Sorry to scare you."

I force myself to my feet and go into the kitchen, finding cold coffee in the coffeemaker. I zap it in the microwave, then sit at the table and chug it.

Once I'm sufficiently buzzed, I call Rambo.

"Nic, what up?"

"Nothing. I'm bored. You?"

"Shopping." Which is a typical Rambo Sunday activity. "Slide's here too. Sounds like you need to get out. We'll finish up here, then we'll come and get you. You don't gotta be home for dinner, do you?"

"No."

"Good."

"Wait—you're not gonna call Zin, are you?" I ask.

"I wasn't planning on it. He hates shopping. Why? You guys get in a fight?"

"What'd he do?" Slide puts in.

"Nothing. I just—I don't want to see him today."

"You the boss, Nic," Rambo says. "We'll see you in a few."

I take a shower, put on some decent clothes, and wait for my ride. When the Nissan pulls up, I put on a cheerful front, but I know I'm not convincing. The guys prod me to find out what happened between me and Zin. I tell them his arrogance about breakdancing is getting to be too much.

"I'll be honest with you," Rambo says. "Zin called. Once he found out we were seeing you, he made me promise to give you a message."

My eyes widen. *What is Zin willing to say in front of these guys?*

"He said that you got no choice but to hear him out, so you can expect to see him soon."

"That sounds like a threat!" Slide says. "Are you sure this is about breakdancing?"

I don't say anything.

It does sound like a threat.

We spend the day visiting outlet stores on Long Island, then hit Pizza Hut's buffet for dinner. By the time I get home, it's eleven o'clock and I'm beyond tired. I'm what British people called shattered, in more ways than one.

My plan is to put on a movie in the den and hopefully fall asleep there. That way, if I get a visitor at my window, I won't be there. Plus, it doesn't hurt that the den has a lock on the door.

I head upstairs to my room, flick the light on. I didn't realize I'd been holding my breath; I half expected Zin to be standing there. Grabbing my duvet, pillow, and pajamas, I go downstairs and set myself up on the brown leather couch in the den, switching on the TV. I hear footsteps on the stairs. Dad appears in the doorway.

"You're planning to sleep down here?"

"I'll probably go upstairs later. I just want to get comfortable."

"All right. Night, honey."

"Night, Dad."

Once I hear him go back upstairs, I mute the TV and turn

off the lights. My mind is going in circles, and as exhausted as I am, I can't shut it off. So I resolve just to rest, if not sleep, and wonder if I'll ever sleep peacefully again.

A rush of cold air envelops me. I open my eyes.

The blue and white glow of the TV fills the room. It's the time of night where some stations stop broadcasting; there's only fuzz on the screen.

Zin is standing in the middle of the room. I know his silhouette. A scream rises in me but fades just as quickly. He's not here to hurt me.

"You're beautiful when you sleep."

I sit up, gathering the duvet around me.

"And when you're awake." He moves, only to switch on a lamp. It takes my eyes a few seconds to adjust. When they do, it's just him. Beautiful. Solid.

"You can see I'm not here to hurt you."

"I don't want you here."

"I know. But leaving you alone wasn't an option, now that you know about us. I think it's best—we *all* think it's best—if you understand."

"So that I don't go to the police?"

"You're smart enough to know that you'd only be making yourself look crazy."

"Am I crazy?"

"No. You're not crazy, and I'm not evil. Deep down, you know that."

Maybe he's right. Maybe underneath my fear, I know he can't be evil.

"We're immortals, Nic. What I told you was true."

"Who's 'we'?"

"All the full-timers at Evermore. Me, Carlo, Viola, Mig, Richard, Gabriel. And Daniella. We've been together for a while. The magician changed us all, made us what we are."

Who you are, I want to correct him again, but I don't. A thought occurs to me. "Carlo's the magician."

"Yes, he is. How did you know?"

"I had . . . a weird dream. What gives you the right to take someone's soul?"

"We take souls to stay alive. But we only take them from people who are dying anyway. And we don't take the soul of just anyone; some souls are very strong and can't be absorbed, even at the time of death. We take damaged, diseased souls—those of drug addicts or hardcore alcoholics. Addiction pierces holes in the soul, Nic. Those souls are easy to absorb."

"Souls like my brother's?"

His eyes drop. I don't expect him to answer. But then he raises his head and nods. "Like your brother's, if he were to overdose."

I take a shuddering breath. "You're stopping people's souls from going on to the next stage."

"I'm sorry to break this to you, but there is no heaven, no other side. The souls we take are lucky, because they can live on inside us. Most souls, at death, just dissipate."

"How do you know?"

"I've been around a long time."

"You haven't answered my question."

"I just know this is the way it is."

"Sounds like you have a God complex."

"Maybe. The way we survive isn't easy to accept. But the alternative is to let yourself die a slow, horrible death—to let your body decay right in front of you like a corpse would in the ground. It's not an option. Listen, Nic. What I told you about my past, the confusion . . . it was all true. I just didn't tell you there were others like me. I had no right to share their secret."

I smile humorlessly. "Lonely immortal, huh? Roaming the world by yourself? I'm the only one you can talk to?"

The remorse in his eyes changes to bitterness. "Maybe one day you'll understand."

"I don't need to understand. You don't need to tell me all of this. Why are you?"

"We thought it was best if I explained it to you. Nobody wants to scare you. In fact, we'd like to see you back at Evermore next week."

I blink. "You want me to go back there?"

"We're all human, Nic. There's never been a mortal that we could let in before. Now that you know, you don't have to run away."

"Keep your friends close and your enemies closer, huh?"

"We're no threat to you or anyone else."

"Except to someone who has a weak soul and is dying."

"You're brave." He takes a step closer, touches my face with the back of his fingers. "At least it shows you're not scared anymore."

I swallow, avoiding his gaze. I wouldn't say I'm not scared. But I wouldn't say I've been scared off, either.

"Do you have a name? People like you, I mean?"

"In the Far East, we're called Jiang Shi."

"What about here?"

"There's no name for us here, no mythology."

"Could you take my soul?"

"Only if you wanted me to. So you're safe."

"Not even Carlo the magician could take it?"

"Not even Carlo."

"How do you know my soul is so strong?"

"I can see it." He sits down beside me. "I'm seeing it right now."

I feel exposed, but I don't know which part of me to cover up. "How?"

"You know what they say about the eyes."

We are staring at each other. I feel the strangest sensation in my chest. It's as if my soul is lifting.

"Nic, do you remember when we first met, and you were wearing those contact lenses? It drove me nuts. I couldn't see you. I needed to see you."

He *is* seeing me. And I am seeing him. And it's way too intense.

I have to look away. The sensation in my chest eases.

"So that night, you didn't guide my attacker's soul . . . you took it."

He nods.

"What does that even feel like?"

He's silent, as if he's pondering the question. "I'll tell you if you really want to know."

"I want to know."

He takes a breath. "It's pain and ecstasy at the same time. You struggle with it, try to bring it into you, and the closer it gets, the sweeter it feels. And when the soul is inside you, it's still fighting, but you know you've won. You feel ten feet tall with the strength of a hundred men. But the high doesn't last. Within hours your energy crashes and you get physically sick for a couple of days as your body fights to control the soul inside you. It squirms and kicks like a baby fighting to get out of its mother's belly. Eventually it stops fighting. It knows who's in control." A pulse flickers in his eyes. "I hope I didn't scare you."

"You did." But I can't look away.

UNDAUNTED

Everything has changed, and nothing has changed.

The next day as I sit in my classes, copy notes, and suffer through group work, Zin still owns my thoughts like he owns a dance floor.

I feel like I'm living in an alternate reality where the surface of life is the same, but the underbelly is different. It's confusing, maddening. But the one thing I know for sure is that Zin is not evil. He does what he must to survive. It doesn't matter if it's right or wrong. I doubt even the strongest person could refuse to take a soul if it would result in their own horrid death.

I wonder how Zin can be so sure that there's nothing after we die—that our souls dissipate, that it's the end. How could he know, when he hasn't died himself?

I have so many questions. The more I think of, the more spring up.

Second period, we're given time in the computer lab to work on our philosophy essays. Sweet. What was it he'd called people like him again? It was some Chinese word sounding like "jengshi."

I type in the word: *Jengshi.*

The search engine brings up the last names of a few people, nothing significant.

I try it as two words. Google asks: Did you mean *Jiang Shi?* I click that.

The first site I see is all about Asian folklore. I scroll down.

Jiang Shi. Translation: Stiff corpse. Also known as Chinese zombies. A popular fixture of Hong Kong horror films, the Jiang Shi are resurrected corpses that stay alive not through traditional vampirical blood drinking, but by absorbing the souls of their victims. Sometimes mistakenly referred to as Chinese vampires.

Beside the entry, there are pictures from horror films showing zombielike creatures with hideously long arms, tongues, and fingernails resulting from rigor mortis. I cringe.

Zin isn't one of those monsters. Whoever he is, he isn't *that.*

Sadness sweeps through me. I just want Zin to be the Zin I know. Not some supernatural *brought-back-from-the-brink-of-death* person. Not something there isn't a name for in English.

But there's no point wishing for something that isn't possible.

I skim over a few websites, but there's nothing helpful. Most of it is about the role of the Jiang Shi in horror films from the eighties. I find a paper from a film student saying that the Jiang Shi are usually dressed in military uniforms in films to symbolize state oppression. There is a picture of a government official with pasty white skin and blood dripping from his eyes with the caption: "I will eat your soul."

"Ick!" a voice says behind me.

I jump in my seat. Ms. Rankin is staring at the screen and making faces. "Were you planning to change your topic to horror films, Nicole?"

"No." I am more than happy to click away.

Breaker practice that night is oddly normal. I already explained to the guys that Zin and I have resolved our differences and are on good terms again. They seem relieved. At heart, the Toprocks are a peace-loving group, except on the dance floor.

My arm is back to normal and seems to have no permanent nerve damage. I'm still avoiding putting too much weight on it, though. The guys get on my case for favoring it, but I know they don't blame me.

After practice, I'm about to get a ride home with Rambo when Zin asks if I'll stay for a while. "We've got a few things to sort out," he explains. "I'll get you a cab."

I agree, and the guys are off. When the door closes, Zin turns to me and smiles. "Privacy, finally. I've missed you."

I feel a rush of excitement. But I remind myself that Zin always speaks this way to me, like I'm the special guest at the party.

"There are no secrets between us anymore, Nic. I can tell you anything you want to know. Or I could tell you nothing. Whatever you want."

"I have some questions."

He cocks a brow. "I have the feeling that's an understatement."

"I was on the Internet today and looked up Jiang Shi."

His eyes widen. "Damn it, I should have warned you. All that stuff is—"

"Bullshit. I know."

He looks relieved. "We're depicted as back-from-the-dead zombies or blood-sucking vampires, but we're nothing like that. We're flesh-and-blood humans like anyone else."

"I have a question, and I can't believe I never asked you this before."

"Go for it."

"On the dance floor, you have to hold back, right? You can't show us everything you can actually do, because it wouldn't seem human?"

"I wouldn't go that far. I can't fly or anything. I just have extra strength and speed. It's generated from the fact that I'm carrying several souls inside me besides my own."

"Show me."

"Show you?"

"How high can you really jump?"

"The ceiling's too low to show you."

"You're serious, aren't you?"

"Of course." He puts on the music.

"Shouldn't we move the furniture?"

"No need." He grins. "I'm light on my feet when I need to be."

The next track is k-os's latest hip-hop beat. Zin does a couple of slides before dropping into eight steps. He works a couple of circles, going faster and faster until my eyes can hardly keep up with him.

But he's just getting started. He's doing headspins so fast my vision literally blurs. He jumps out of it. Although he's sweating, he doesn't look winded. He seems to enjoy my awestruck expression. "Have you seen the movie *The Matrix*?"

"Yeah." I blink. He just ran up the wall and bounced off the ceiling. "Could you do that again?"

He does, running up the wall, hitting two feet on the ceiling before dropping to his feet.

He's standing in front of me, grinning. "That move's good cardio."

"Wow. Are you sure you're human?"

"I'm sweating, aren't I? I didn't do anything supernatural. That was all speed."

"You'd win Dance America in a heartbeat."

"I know. It wouldn't be fair. I'm not even sure if battling is fair, but I try very hard to keep my moves within the normal range. I don't let myself do anything that I wouldn't have done in my days as an acrobat."

"If I could do things like that, I'd show the world and make tons of money."

He laughs. "You wouldn't cheat in competition, Nic."

"Wouldn't I? Dance America's a hundred grand. I could donate half of it to charity. That would satisfy my conscience."

"No, it wouldn't. Your soul is too pure. It's one of the amazing things about you."

Amazing things about *me*? It's so ridiculous, I have to laugh.

He laughs too, but I'm not sure if we're laughing at the same thing.

"What now? I'm not working tonight." He reaches out his hand. "Want to roam?"

"Sure."

The streets of the Village are Monday-night quiet, with the occasional homeless person huddling in a corner or disaffected spouse smoking on a balcony. I like this neighborhood, but only because Zin's presence lends it safety. With Zin by my side, I could go anywhere.

The lyrics of an old song come into my head. *I can go where no one else can go. I know what no one else knows.*

Walking next to Zin lends a different aura to the darkened streets and shadowy old buildings. An aura of magic.

"I love New York." He manages to say it without sounding cliché. "I wouldn't want to stay forever, but I love it."

It's hard not to let my New Yorker pride come up. "You've lived in all different parts of the world. Have you found a better city than this?"

"It's not about better. Every city has a different energy, a different pulse. New York is the perfect city to be involved in the club business. The perfect place to breakdance. Its pulse is fast and frenetic. But I've loved other places for different reasons. I love towns that connect waterways and mountain ranges. Their pulse is the steady pulse of the land, the heartbeat of nature. I can spend years in those places."

I'm afraid to ask, but I force myself. "How long do you think you'll be in New York?"

"We do ten years in every place. It's easiest that way. We've been here for six."

Four more years. The idea of knowing Zin for only four more years is unbearable. Where will the light come from then?

"Does the thought of leaving . . ." *make you sad*, I want to ask. But he'll know why I'm asking, so I don't say it. "Where will you go next?"

"We don't decide until very soon before we leave."

"Does it have to be every ten years like clockwork? I'm sure people wouldn't notice you're not aging. People can stay looking so young these days."

He smiles. "We feel it's best. It's not always easy, though, if we have attachments." But he's not looking at me as he says it. He's looking straight up at the sky, where his gaze inevitably strays. "And there are places in this world that need us more than New York City. Coming here was an indulgence, and we never indulge ourselves for long."

"So after this, you might go become aid workers or something?"

"We go where we're needed. The last few places . . . burned us out pretty badly."

"I had no idea you used your immortality that way—to help people. I just thought . . . I guess I hadn't given it much thought."

"Running a club is great for a few years, but it wouldn't give us any lasting satisfaction. And when you've lived a long time, satisfaction is hard to come by. Especially considering the way we survive."

"It bothers you, doesn't it?"

"Yeah." He kicks a pebble.

"Obviously you and the Jiang Shi are giving back to the world, though. It should balance out, don't you think?"

"I don't know. Maybe I'll find out one day."

We're walking through a depressed area, with boarded-up buildings and graffiti. Normally I'd be looking over my shoulder, but not now. It's freeing.

"Must be wonderful to go wherever you like without being scared of anything," I say.

"It is, but the newness of it wears off. For you, I bet it would be a rush, especially being a girl."

"Yeah, there's that part. My girl-strength didn't exactly come to my rescue a few weeks ago."

"I didn't mean to get you thinking about that."

"I was already thinking about it." I look at him. "So what happens if an immortal gets hurt? *Can* you get hurt?"

"We can, but the energy inside us allows us to regenerate. The combined light of the souls inside us is powerful—the more souls we have inside us, the more powerful we are. So if Carlo were to get hurt, he'd heal more quickly than I would. He's the oldest of us, with the most souls."

"Even diseased souls have this energy that can heal you?"

"All human souls do. You see that guy over there?"

His vision is sharp. I might not have spotted the guy. He's a few yards down, a gray figure against a gray doorway.

"Yeah, I see him."

119

ALLISON VAN DIEPEN

"His soul is a mess. But it still has light. I can see it from here."

"Looks like he's talking to himself."

"You would think so. But his soul has been taken over by an entity—a negative energy that feeds on broken souls."

"You're saying he's possessed?"

He nods. "There are worse things than Jiang Shi out there, trust me." At my look of alarm, he says, "But your soul is strong, so you'll never have to know them."

"Is there anything that can be done for him?"

"He can push the entity out if he wants to. But he might not know the difference between himself and the entity anymore." As we pass the guy, Zin drops a couple of dollars into the can in front of him.

"Every dollar's a choice," I quote him.

"Every moment is a choice. For the record, I've seen guys on Wall Street with worse souls than his."

"Can you switch it off so you don't have to see souls all the time?"

"No. But it doesn't bother me nearly as much as it used to. You get desensitized. It's not what's outside me that's the hard part."

We come to a small fenced-in park. He climbs over the short fence; I do too. It's a little oasis of snow and icy-limbed trees, a winter paradise in the middle of the city.

"What's the hard part?" I ask.

"The souls inside me. It's a constant mental fight to keep them down. Pesky ones can bother the hell out of you."

I look up at him, the moonlight icing his hair. A shiver comes over me. "But they can't take you over, right?"

His teeth glint white in the darkness. "No. Carlo trains us to fortify our minds and souls so we can control the souls we've absorbed."

"Good, because . . ."

"Chris Harris will never take me over, I promise you. Persistent guy, but weak."

"Chris Harris—was that his name?"

"That's what he was called. Souls don't usually identify themselves by name."

"This is creeping me out."

"You have no reason to be scared. I would protect you with my soul." He cups my face. His hands are warm despite the cold. "You remind me of how precious life is."

I call in an anonymous tip, naming Chris Harris as my attacker.

It's the right thing to do. He must have a family somewhere. A family that deserves to know.

Two days later a cop calls me with details. Chris Harris was known on the streets as Main—like maniac, not Main Street. He had a long rap sheet with arrests for drug possession, assault, and B and E.

He was from Colorado. Land of mountains and streams and

postcards. I wonder if he grew up in a city or a small town. I wonder when his trouble started. I wonder when his soul began to deteriorate.

I wonder if Zin's soul can save his, at least for a while.

I'm having a last-minute freak-out. I thought I was ready to return to Evermore, but now I'm not sure. Zin is one thing. I trust him. A whole group of soul-stealing Jiang Shi is another. Maybe I should've thought about this more.

Zin tugs my hand as we round the corner toward Evermore. "C'mon, Nic. They're all just like me. There's no reason to get upset."

"I'm not upset. I'm just sweating profusely."

He has the nerve to laugh.

"H-hey guys," I greet Mig and Richard. Mig gives me a big smile, followed by a wink. My eyes widen, and he bursts out laughing. Richard nods his head formally.

Viola greets me with the usual air kisses. It hits me that she's probably old enough to be my great-great-grandmother. She begins to chatter like she always does. Her warmth calms me. I try not to think about what I saw her do last week.

It was survival, I remind myself, nothing more.

Then I see Carlo approach, and my whole body stiffens. Carlo the magician, the oh-so-powerful one, He Who Screws with Life and Death.

"Hello, Raven."

There's that name again.

"Hi."

I don't stick around to chat. I spot customers who need attending to, and I hurry to take their orders.

When I bring my first order up to Zin, he's still got the annoying smirk on his face. I decide to ignore it.

"Are the guys coming tonight?" I ask.

"I talked to Rambo a couple of hours ago. He said they might stop by later. They're going to a club in midtown to make money off tourists."

"What if the Spinheads or the Double You's show up?"

"We're not ready to battle yet. We're worried you might mess up the arm. A few more weeks and we'll be good to go." He loads up my tray.

By one a.m. I'm exhausted, and even though I told myself I'd do some dancing on my break, I decide to go up to the balcony for a breather. I lean on the banister overlooking the dance floor.

A voice emerges from the darkness. "You don't have to fear us, Raven."

Carlo walks up, leaning on the banister beside me. "I know it's a lot to take in. The universe as you know it has shifted. The impossible has become possible. Zin trusts you, and so do I." His gaze sweeps the club below. "I want you to know that there is no need for fear. You are safe with us. As safe as if you were one of us."

"I know."

"You can't know. But you will, in time. I hope Zinadin has given you no reason to fear me."

"He said you were powerful . . . but not in a bad way."

At that, he smiles. "Zinadin may have described me as a magician. Most people have over the years. It seems to be a term that fits with popular culture. But I can't say I've ever made magic. I'm just acquainted with the science of the soul. I've learned that many things are possible if the universe cooperates."

I have no clue what to say, so I choose lame humor. "So you can turn me into a rabbit?"

"No, but I can turn you into a Jiang Shi."

I flinch.

"That was a miserable attempt to tease you. Obviously humor is not my forte. I came up here because I wanted to put you at ease, believe it or not. I want you to be happy working here."

It's true that he could be saying this because I know his secret now, but I think his caring is genuine.

"Evermore isn't what I thought it was, but I'm still in love with this place. It still feels like home."

"Good. I am pleased that you know about us, Raven. It feels right, does it not?"

I nod. I feel privileged to be the one mortal they trust.

We both gaze down at the action below, the dancers winding up to a frenzied pace. His sleeve brushes mine, and I have no need to move away. I feel close to him.

"I understand our Zinadin is introducing you to how we live. I extend you that same invitation. Ask me anything, and I will tell you."

"Thanks." I don't know what I've done to deserve this, but I'm glad. "I always want to know more."

A ghost of a smile. "I thought you might."

MYSTERY
EXPLORE

Nothing ever goes back to normal. All that happens is your concept of normal changes.

Like with Zin and the Jiang Shi. As weeks go by, the new reality sinks in, and they seem normal to me, just as normal as anyone else. They just happen to be older and wiser. Zin says you don't live hundreds of years without gaining wisdom, even if you were a dumbass to begin with—not that any of them were. Far from it, it seems.

Which makes me wonder why Carlo changed the people he did. It's hard to believe that he changed people randomly. The more I hear, the more I'm convinced he chose special people. Viola mentioned that Zin had been an acrobat famous "all over the Middle East." That's rather more than the carnival act he mentioned.

But Zin's background is humble compared to the others: Gabriel led a black regiment during the French Revolution;

Mig was a Spanish explorer; Richard was a knight in Elizabethan times; Viola was an accomplished poet in Georgian England who wrote under a male pseudonym. And Daniella, well, she's Carlo's sister. Changing her was a no-brainer.

I ask Viola about all of this one night as we're getting changed for our shift.

"Carlo favors strong people, physically and mentally. All of the men in our group could defend us if need be. And they have."

"What about you? He must value literature, too."

She laughs. "You could say that. I certainly wasn't the typical female of my day. People used to call me an original, and it wasn't a compliment. Society didn't exactly approve of me."

"Because you were a poet?"

"No, that came later. Initially it was because I refused to marry one of my many suitors, and my mother, bless her heart, wouldn't force me to marry someone I didn't love. And then, when I was nineteen, I got caught in a compromising situation with one of my brother's friends . . . it ruined me. I was shunned by society, and my prospects for marrying well were dashed." She grins. "Best thing that ever happened to me."

"Seriously?"

"Oh, yes. I withdrew from all the games of London high society and focused on my dreams of writing and traveling the Continent. During my travels in Italy, I met Carlo. He was an

Italian count, incredibly dashing." Her expression goes dreamy. "We fell in love."

"You and Carlo? I had no idea."

"Being with Carlo was . . . bliss. There was no doubt in my mind that we would marry and be together forever. But on the night I expected him to propose, he ended the relationship."

"I guess he had no choice."

"Right, but of course, he didn't tell me the real reason he couldn't marry me. I thought it was because I'd made the mistake of telling him about my reputation; I was a fool. I left Italy, devastated. A year later, when I became very ill, I wrote him a letter of farewell. He came to me immediately. And when I was near death, he changed me."

"Wow. How long were you together?"

"About a century. Since then, on and off."

"A century? That's the longest relationship I've ever heard of." She laughs. "It was long, but wonderful."

"Why did you end it then?"

"We didn't want to tire of each other, so we decided to take an extended break. We'll get back together one day. A great love can survive centuries, and that's what Carlo and I have."

An image of Zin comes to mind. I could imagine spending centuries with him. There are some people you can never get tired of. Some people are eternal.

If only I had that kind of deal with Zin. If only I knew our time would come.

But that's Viola's love story, not mine.

Tonight, for the first time, I'm invited to one of Carlo's Sunday dinners.

When I walk in, I feel deflated. I thought I'd be the only non–Jiang Shi there, but it turns out several of the Jiang Shi have brought their friends.

Carlo's place is a black-and-white maze of rooms. It must have at least four bedrooms, or maybe the mirrors on certain walls make it look bigger than it is. The living room is minimalist, with soft black seating and white walls. Right out of a style magazine.

Zin isn't here yet, and Viola is engrossed in conversation with a guy (I imagine it's her boyfriend), so I take a seat on the couch beside Richard. He's as tall and strong as Mig, but not at all gregarious, and with a formality that's not very twenty-first-century. He's hardly said two words to me since I came to Evermore.

"Hey." I smile.

"Hello."

We sit in silence for a couple of minutes. I rack my brain for something to say. "I hear you knew Queen Elizabeth the First," I say quietly. "What was she like?"

"Crusty, but well respected."

"Crusty? You mean she was bitchy?"

"I mean she was crusty. She wore far too much foundation. Back then they used white lead paint. By the end of the day it would get all cracked and crusty. It was grotesque."

"Ick."

Carlo asks me what I would like to drink. Carlo serving *me*? Now this is a nice change. I ask for a gin and tonic, a fairly adult drink. He brings it back in a minute.

"Thanks, Carlo. You're an excellent host."

He smiles.

A few more people arrive, and Richard and I are joined on the couch by Gabriel, who brings with him a quiet intensity so different from Richard's quiet calmness. When Gabriel starts talking politics, it hits me that our interaction has never been anything but music-related until now.

"And if it doesn't change, we're going to have another Civil War," he says. "*This* century."

"The next major war will not be within this country," Richard says. "World War Three will force the West to unite."

I sip my drink, wishing I'd chosen something fruity. I'd rather not hear this WWIII talk. It scares me. Which probably doesn't make sense, since by the end of the century I'll be dead, and these guys won't.

Daniella perches on the side of the couch, her slim, bearded boyfriend standing next to her holding a martini. I hear he's an academic type named James, but she hasn't bothered to introduce him to me. "Did I hear something about World War Three?" she asks.

"It's coming," Richard says. "One could argue it's already begun in the Middle East."

Daniella raises an eyebrow. "Ever the cynic. What is it with you guys?" She turns to James. "Am I the only eternal optimist?"

"I'm an optimist," I say. "At least, I try to be."

Daniella shrugs her left shoulder, which is her way of acknowledging my existence. I'd prefer that she completely ignore me rather than give me this patronizing little shrug.

I excuse myself and go to the kitchen, where Carlo is tossing veggies in a pan. His kitchen is exactly what I would have expected—sleek, state-of-the-art appliances, black and silver.

"Smells good. Can I help with anything?"

"That's okay. I'm a well-oiled machine, as they say. But thank you, Raven."

"Thanks for inviting me."

"You are one of the family."

I feel the little hairs on the back of my neck stand up. Something about the way he says it makes me nervous. I force a smile. "Yeah, yeah. I'm sure you say that to all the mortals."

"Actually, I don't." The pan sizzles as he tosses the vegetables.

I feel an inexplicable panic. Then I realize: Of course he

doesn't say it to all the mortals; I'm the only mortal who knows about them.

"I'm glad you're okay with me knowing about you guys," I say.

"I trust you completely."

"Thanks. I'm not sure if I've earned that yet, but I appreciate it."

"You didn't have to earn it. I can see your soul."

"Oh, right. So you can see that I'm not the type of person to sell you out to the *Enquirer*."

He looks puzzled. "Who is the enquirer?"

I laugh. I guess he hasn't been in America all that long. "It's just a gossip rag."

"Ah, yes."

I watch him for a while. "I hear you're a world-class cook."

"I've had years of practice. But if your expectations are high, I'm afraid you'll be disappointed."

"I never have high expectations. That way I'm rarely disappointed, or at least, rarely surprised." Maybe it's the buzz from my drink, but I feel like I can ask him anything; he did tell me I could. "I see that a lot of the Jiang Shi are having relationships with mortals. Are you ever worried they'll get too serious?"

"They know they will have to disengage at the appropriate time. Most do so well before the time comes. It's the nature of most romantic relationships that they will not last."

"What about you—do you have relationships with women?"

A black eyebrow arches. "You're curious tonight."

"Sorry."

"No need." He puts a lid over the pan and leaves it to simmer. Approaching the marble island where I'm sitting, he steeples his fingers. "I enjoy the company of women. I simply prefer to keep it in the realm of dating. Fortunately, my way isn't unusual these days. Women are disappointed, but never surprised."

"That's sad."

"I do what's best for all concerned."

I remember Zin's words that horrible night he rejected me. *I'm doing what's best for you.*

Carlo stares into me like he's reading my thoughts. "Most Jiang Shi leave a trail of broken hearts behind them. I try to avoid that. I would not have a serious relationship with a mortal woman."

"Viola said you were together for a while."

"The longest relationship in my rather long lifetime, though I spent thirty years with a woman named Martine."

"You spent that long with a woman who wasn't a Jiang Shi?"

He shakes his head. "She was one of us."

"Where is she now?"

His expression darkens. "Murdered."

"How's that possible?"

"Since you know about the Jiang Shi, you might as well know about our enemies. They are called Heng Te, which means hunters. They are mortals, Chinese scholar-warriors whose goal has been to rid the earth of every last Jiang Shi. Fortunately we have managed to elude them for several generations."

I can't believe this. The Jiang Shi have enemies? It's sickening to think that the Heng Te's purpose is to kill them. The Jiang Shi don't have it easy, and they pay their dues to humanity in any way they can. At least, that's what Zin's been telling me.

"I thought it was impossible to kill a Jiang Shi."

"They can drain every last soul from our bodies. That is the only way to kill us."

"Oh God."

"Don't worry, Raven. All of the Jiang Shi know how to defend themselves. Everyone has been trained and tested."

"Tested for what?" Zin appears in the doorway of the kitchen.

"Syphilis," I say, taking another sip of my drink.

"Syphilis sucks," Zin says. "Ask Mig. He had it before he was changed."

"I hope this won't become our dinner conversation," Carlo says.

It's hard to picture Carlo doing anything half-assed. Like our dinner—it's a traditional Italian meal with a variety of veggies, three kinds of fish, and homemade pasta. The Jiang Shi attack the food like it's their last meal, the same way Zin always has. I guess having extra souls inside you boosts your appetite.

I have Carlo on one side of me (at the head of the table, no surprise) and Viola's boyfriend, Kirk, on the other. Kirk is a pro motocross racer who tours the country sponsored by some big company I've never heard of. He's good-looking in a rugged way, but rough around the edges, and not someone I could picture sophisticated Viola falling in love with. But then, maybe that's the appeal.

The sadness of it strikes me. Am I better off not being with Zin the way I crave? Every time I look at him across the table, I know I'm not. If he gives me a chance one day, I'll take it. Even if it ends in heartbreak. *Knowing* it will end in heartbreak.

I realize I'm not the only one watching Zin. Daniella is too, beneath her dark eyelashes. She's doing it subtly enough that her date doesn't seem to notice. But I notice. I can't believe I haven't sensed it before, but then, I've rarely been in close proximity to both of them.

Daniella is in love with Zin. Whoa. I'm not ready to deal with this.

If I can see it, Zin must see it too. Are they going to get together? It would be the perfect match; they're both Jiang Shi.

Maybe they've *already* gotten together. Of course. This group has been together for such a long time that any attraction would have played out years ago. Obviously Daniella still has feelings for him.

It's amazing how so much can become clear in a second.

It was hard enough to accept that he had a serious girlfriend once—even if it was two hundred years ago—but a relationship with Daniella? Suddenly my dinner seems less appealing.

I turn to Carlo. "Are you reading my mind or something?"

His smile is gentle. "It's easier to read your face. I'm watching you respond to your intuition. Intuition is everything, isn't it? You are correct, Raven."

"They used to be . . . a couple?"

"For a short time—five years, perhaps. A one-night stand, by our standards."

"What happened?"

"Ask him. I'm sure he will tell you. It is so long ago now."

So Zin and Daniella are not some eternal couple like Carlo and Viola.

Thank God.

Ex-girlfriends are like car wrecks.

You shouldn't want to know the details, but you do.

We're in an empty corner of the train on orange plastic seats. At the other end of the car, a group of teens in preppy getups are being loud and obnoxious. I wonder if I'm really of the same generation as them, or if it's some cosmic mix-up.

"So you and Daniella, huh? Way back when?"

He doesn't look happy. "Carlo told you."

"He confirmed it. But I noticed her looking at you."

He sighs. "I'd prefer to forget it ever happened."

"Sorry. I know it's none of my business."

"It's not that. I guess I didn't tell you because . . . knowing my life was saved because of a crush isn't something I'm proud of."

"Are you saying Carlo changed you because Daniella had a *crush* on you?"

"That's exactly what I'm saying. I wasn't a knight in the Elizabethan court. I wasn't a war hero. I was just an entertainer."

"A famous one, from what I've heard."

"I wasn't famous then. I was a popular act at the local carnival, nothing more. Carlo and the Jiang Shi were in the audience one day, and apparently Daniella claimed it was love at first sight. I'd call it an infatuation, since we hadn't actually spoken."

To my surprise, I feel for Daniella. Who are we to say if it was love or not? When I first saw Zin, an intense emotion came over me. If Daniella felt something similar, I can't blame her for calling it love.

"I got sick around that time, and she asked Carlo to change me. After I was changed, my life was turned upside down. I left my village, met up with the Jiang Shi, and got together with Daniella."

"But you didn't love her?"

"No. I tried to convince myself that I did. It would've been a lot easier to love a Jiang Shi. I didn't want to be alone back then."

Back then. He wants to be alone now?

"I'm grateful to Daniella. She helped me learn how to live as a Jiang Shi. She loved me even though I'd done nothing to deserve it, even though she knew that I never really loved her back. I know she can be cold at times, but she's a good person."

"Must've been a terrible situation for both of you."

"I was too wrapped up in myself to notice her suffering." The side of his mouth goes up without humor. "I actually resented her for asking Carlo to change me. I didn't want to be a Jiang Shi. I wanted my other life back. I know it sounds irrational; I'd have been dead if I hadn't been changed. But I wasn't at my most rational then—it's your stop."

He catches the door before it closes, holding it open so I can slip through. We climb the stairs leading us out of the station.

I realize that Daniella and I have more in common than I thought. As hard as it is for me to love Zin and not be with him, her situation—being with him but knowing he didn't love her—must've been worse.

My neighborhood is silent except for a strong wind rustling the trees. Above us, the stars are muted and far away. I wish I could feel the warmth of Zin's hand over mine. But he only takes my hand when he's leading me somewhere.

"I always wondered if Carlo regretted changing me. He

spent centuries protecting her, and then I came along and broke her heart."

"He couldn't protect her from being human. Heartbreak is a part of that." I glance at him. Sometimes just being by his side is enough, but other times, like now, the distance between us is unbearable.

"I guess it is."

"Carlo couldn't regret changing you, because he knows you."

"He's said many times that he sees me as a son. But sometimes I wonder if he really does."

"I'm sure Carlo wouldn't say it if it weren't true."

"That's the mystery of the magician. You can know him two hundred years and not know him at all."

SOUL HATH SPOKEN

When I get home from school the next day, Mom is in the living room reading a magazine. I have the feeling she's been waiting for me.

"Nicole."

Uh-oh.

"Josh called." She walks toward me, eyes swollen from tears.

Josh. The ghost. I've hardly thought of him in weeks. I was fine with that. Happy with that.

I consider running—to my room, out the front door. I can't choose, and so I go nowhere.

"Mom, I'm—"

"He said he never called. That you made it up. I told him you wouldn't lie to us and that he must've forgotten calling. Then he told me what happened at the club."

I drop my eyes.

"How could you let those bouncers beat him up? Isn't

his life miserable enough already?" She starts to cry.

I try to hug her, but she moves away.

"They didn't beat him up, Mom. He got all crazy, so they had to take him outside."

"He says you humiliated him in front of his friends. Your brother feels bad enough about his life without you being so hard on him."

"I was just trying to help."

"*Help?* He says you accused him of manipulating us out of money. He was so hurt that he refused to call to get the money we'd promised him. They kicked him out of the rooming house because he couldn't pay the rent. He called me from a shelter."

A lump burns my throat.

Even if I could say it, *sorry* seems pointless now.

Her eyes are huge, magnified by tears. "I can't believe you would lie to us and tell us he was okay. I'm just beside myself, Nicole. I knew Josh was manipulative. I never thought you were too."

I just stand there, waiting for her eyes to let go of me.

Then she's crying again. I wish she'd go back to the anger. If she wants to yell at me, I've got plenty of anger to throw back at her. But I can't yell at her tears.

I run up to my room, collapsing on my bed. All I wanted to do was protect her and Dad. Why can't she understand that?

Everything is so fucked up. So completely and utterly fucked up.

I wish I could do something, take something, to make this pain go away.

But no, that's Josh's style. He's the addict.

I can't self-destruct.

I have no more tears. I need to go somewhere. I need to escape.

I call up Zin. "Can I come over?"

"Of course. Are you okay?"

"No. It hit the fan."

I ride the subway with my eyes closed, my iPod playing upbeat hip-hop. I crank the music up to drown out the squeaking of the train. The lady next to me gives me a nudge, so I turn it down a little. *Yes, lady, I'm going to be deaf by the time I'm twenty. I've already accepted that.*

When I arrive at his door, Zin hugs me. "You don't look so good, Nic. You haven't eaten, have you?"

"I don't feel like eating."

"At least have some tea." We go to the table, where he's been eating his typical Mediterranean spread. He pours me a cup of tea. "Tell me what happened. Get it out. You'll feel better afterward."

I tell him every last sordid detail. When it's over, I feel lighter for having spewed it all out. Zin isn't looking at me like I'm an evil, selfish being.

"Life sucks that way," he says. "No matter what you do, you can't stop the people you love from suffering."

I nod. It's true. A Jiang Shi would know.

"I wish I could stop you from suffering, Nic. But I can't."

"You help a lot."

I sip my tea. I can't imagine what I'd do without Zin.

"It's five-fifty," he says. "I have to work at nine. Want to catch an early movie, take your mind off things?"

"I don't think I could focus on a movie right now."

"How about a walk?"

"Okay."

It's dusk. Dark masses of cloud blanket the sky, eerily reflecting the city lights. Zin walks faster than usual, making me strain to keep up. I know that he's doing it on purpose, so that I'm walking faster than I'm thinking.

At the river, we look out at the rippling waves. The wind floods my eyes and makes them water. My hair flies every which way, blinding me.

Zin tries to tame it, tucking the hair behind my ears before it goes flying again. We laugh together. And suddenly, from the sadness of an hour ago, I'm looking into his beautiful face, and I feel joy.

He gazes into my eyes. And for a moment I think he might love me too.

"Dear Nic, you amaze me."

His lips close over mine. Like two electrical wires searing together, our energy sparks. I feel the cells of my body coming alive.

There's fire here, and we're coaxing it into an inferno, breathing each other's breath and delving into each other's mouths. My body is pressed against his, my arms around his neck, my hands in his hair. The fire, I realize, is his, in his lips, in his soul, and I'm clamoring to get closer to it, to be burned.

I become aware of a burgeoning in my chest. I have the blissful sensation of my soul rising up inside me, as if it's being pulled to the surface.

I open my eyes slightly, seeing my reflection in his eyes—pale face, dark hair whipping around me. I notice a ball of light glowing inside me. But there's something strange within it, like a rip in a brilliant white blanket. It appears to be a void, oozing darkness.

Panicked, I wrench away. His eyes are flashing like Morse code.

"W-what just happened?" I ask.

"Your soul came up to meet mine." He sounds awestruck.

"I think I saw it—my soul."

"You saw yourself as I see you. It's a beautiful soul, isn't it?"

"There's something wrong with it. Something horrible."

"It's okay, Nic. What you saw is the hole. Where your brother used to be."

"I thought you said my soul was strong!"

"It *is* strong. But it's hurting. In the center of everyone's soul is love. The love we have for others, the love others have for us. In your soul, you're missing Josh. You're missing your family before it was shattered."

I can't believe I have a hole in my soul. A nothing. A void. How could I have been walking around with it and not even know?

"Nic, the first time I saw you without your contact lenses, I saw your soul, in all its pain and beauty. I convinced myself I could help you heal. But I guess all I did was distract you from the pain. I'm sorry."

"How do I heal it then?" I cross my arms over my chest, as if something could seep out of the hole. "I can't make Josh better. I can't make my family okay again."

"Changing the circumstances isn't the cure. Neither is filling it with somebody else."

I blink. "Are you saying I tried to fill it with you?"

His eyes are sad. "Don't you see? I wanted you to fill it with me. I couldn't help myself." He turns away, hands curling around the railing.

I feel sick. So sick. "Are you saying I've been using you to fill up my soul?"

His eyes don't stray from the waves. "Only you know the truth."

"But obviously you can see things that I can't. You see *every-*

thing, don't you? How could you see that hole inside me and not say anything?"

"I didn't think I was supposed to. You carry your pain like everyone else does."

"But it's *horrible*." I think of the hole, the nothingness, and I want to erase it from my memory. "I'm just another sick soul, aren't I?"

"Not to me."

Tears are streaming down my cheeks. He turns to me, touches the side of my face, eyes filled with tenderness. "It'll be okay, Nic."

"No, it won't." I dash away my tears. "Maybe we . . . shouldn't do this. I'm just using you to fill up my soul anyway. Right?"

He doesn't say anything. I'm waiting for him to talk me out of it, but he doesn't utter a word.

"I'm going home." I start walking, and he walks beside me.

"Alone," I say.

He nods, and leaves me to the night.

VELVET SINKING

It was a mistake. I never should have looked so closely into Zin's eyes. I never should have looked into my own soul. But I can't go back. I can't un-know what I know. Even the Jiang Shi, who have conquered life and death, can't go back in time.

Sure, I needed Zin too much. Sure, he was my obsession, my fantasy. But he was my favorite person, the one who made life beautiful. Could he blame me for trying to fill the hole in my soul with him? Was it so wrong?

Two weeks have passed since I looked into my soul, and though I still see Zin often, we feel like strangers. Maybe the kiss didn't mean to him what it did to me. I'm just temporary for him anyway. For him, I'm a potential four-year relationship, a blip on his endless time line.

He doesn't deserve my anger. What I saw isn't his fault. I could have closed my eyes and stayed in peaceful ignorance forever. But no, I wanted to see my soul. Some part of me saw an opportunity to see the truth and took it.

He's right that I was filling my soul with him, but that doesn't mean my love for him isn't real. It is. I know it with the same certainty that recognized the hole inside me. And I know that my love for him is not the sum of his dancing and good looks and charm. My love is the pale boy huddling in the blanket. My love is the rooftop silence.

But it's too late for that.

Carlo prefers candlelight. Though he has two antique lamps in the back of the office, there are only candles within his sight-lines, giving off a soft glow. The room is dark and elegant, like he is—mahogany desk and bookshelf, black leather furniture. When I walk in, he is poring over ledgers, which he keeps in leather-bound books.

"You said you were a soul scientist."

He raises his eyes. "Yes."

"Well, if I have a problem with my soul, maybe you can tell me how to heal it."

"Have a seat, Raven. This is the problem of the hole, I imagine."

"You can see it too?" I hate the thought that I'm an open book for any Jiang Shi to read.

"Yes. Unfortunately, I can't help you close the hole inside

you. I do know, however, that when we ask the universe a question, it tends to give us the opportunity to find the answer. I believe the universe has systems of balance. Keep the question of healing in your mind, and you might find the answer."

"Is it possible there isn't an answer?"

"Of course it is. It's also possible that the answer isn't something you are willing to accept, at least not at the present time."

I feel queasy. "I'm not sure what you mean by that."

"I don't expect you to. Just keep living the question."

"What are we doing tonight?" I ask Rambo on the phone.

"I'm picking up the boys and Kim and we're drinking in the park with some buddies. I'll be at your place at eight."

I'm not big on drinking and can't hold half as much liquor as the guys can, but I don't care because I'm desperate to get out. My house has the kind of sad that oozes from the walls. It's getting to me more than ever. I guess when I relied on Zin, his energy insulated me from it.

It's not warm out by any means, so I put on a black hat and long striped gloves and a sweatshirt under my jacket. Rambo shows up ten minutes late, the car full of cologne and everyone. When we arrive at the park, there's got to be twenty people there. Most of them I know from school.

They're all gathered around the jungle gym on steps and slides and swings.

We sit on the second level of the structure, dangling our legs off the edge. Chen offers me a beer and I accept it, though I'm no fan of beer. There are several random conversations going on. I join one, but it doesn't hold my attention. My mind drifts, and I sip my beer. I can see my breath in the night air.

"You seem down these days." Kim sidles up beside me. "I'm assuming things didn't work out with Zin."

"We have our ups and downs. I guess we're not destined to be a couple."

"I'm sorry to hear that. I hope this isn't my fault. I really thought you guys were a sure thing."

"It's not your fault. We've been spending too much time together anyway. I've been ignoring other things." I glance at her, not sure if I should say more. "Actually, there's a family situation that sometimes gets me down."

"Your brother."

I look at her. "How'd you know?"

"We've spotted him downtown a few times." She doesn't say more, and doesn't have to.

"Oh. I guess I've been kind of embarrassed. I don't really like to talk about it."

"I understand."

I can't believe she and the guys have known this whole time. And I thought I was pulling the wool over their eyes. "Even when I'm not thinking about it, it's still there. It's like . . . a void inside me."

"I know what you mean. My uncle is mentally ill, and he's just holed himself up in his apartment and won't talk to us. It's been hard on the family, especially my mom. They used to be really close."

"I'm sorry. How does your mom deal with it?"

"She accepted that there's nothing she can do. It's still not easy, but it's given her some peace."

"But what about the hole? I mean, the void?"

Kim shrugs. "You have to accept it as part of you. What else can you do? Only your brother can save himself."

I think of the possessed homeless man. According to Zin, even he could save himself if he tried hard enough. That means Josh can too.

But I can't save him.

Viola and I are at a café in downtown Brooklyn stirring milk and sugar into our coffees. A lanky guy comes up, staring at her with this stupidly hopeful expression. "Great day out, huh? Can't wait to take my dogs for a walk."

Viola nods and smiles. I am continually fascinated at how random guys find a way to hit on her wherever she goes.

This is the second time she's asked me to go out for coffee. I hope I'm not a charity case for her. I'd hate to think she's hanging out with me because she sees the hole in my soul.

"Did that guy seriously think he had a chance?" I ask once we're sitting at a table.

"Sure, they all do. It's like playing the lottery. He knows it's a long shot, but he feels he should try."

"Doesn't it get on your nerves?"

"Sometimes. Carlo never liked it."

"Carlo jealous, huh? I could see that."

"He would never admit to being jealous. He just said these men wasted my time and his. He never worried that any of them would make an offer that would tempt me away."

"That's confidence."

"Yes. Confidence is one thing he's not short on. Other things too." She winks.

I nearly choke on my coffee. "Kirk wouldn't want to hear that."

"Kirk would never hear that, trust me. He's jealous enough already. He thinks whenever he's out of town I'm supposed to be calling him twenty-four/seven, pining for him. That just isn't me. A little distance is healthy. It's best for both of us if we don't get too attached."

"Makes sense."

"So you're graduating soon, right? Must be exciting."

"It's a relief. I'm bored of high school. I'm looking forward to moving on."

"What's your plan for next year?"

"I don't know. I'm not sure if I'm going to college just yet."

"Good for you. What a waste of time."

"Seriously?"

"Sure! Why spend the next four precious years of your youth sitting in classrooms, going to bad parties, eating cafeteria food, drinking too much? It's always seemed ridiculous to me. You learn by living your life, not by sitting in a classroom. If there's something you really want to learn about, fine, do it—but unless you're absolutely thirsty for that knowledge, you should stay out here, in the real world."

"Wow. I've never heard anyone put it that way."

"Let's face it, Nicole. You're mortal. I don't mean to depress you, but it's true. You don't have time to waste. Travel the world while you're young and healthy, then come back and get your degree."

"I was thinking about doing that. My parents will be disappointed if I don't go to college right away, but I'm not going to waste the money if I'm not ready."

"What is it you want to study?"

"Psychology, I think. Why people do what they do."

"In a hundred years, everything they're teaching now will

be reversed. The best way to understand people is through experience. Actually, the *best* way is to become a Jiang Shi. Especially when you first turn, you're painfully perceptive— you can see everything, and everyone, so clearly."

"Well, I'm sure I'll never be *that* perceptive."

She smiles. "Count yourself lucky. We all need our illusions."

EBONY BIRD

If dreams tell you something about your subconscious, then I'm screwed.

I'm always dreaming about squawking black birds that hover over horrific disasters—plane crashes, landslides, tsunamis. The dreams are devoid of color, like old movies made with black-and-white film. But the weird thing is, I find myself detached from all the horrors in these dreams, an apathetic spectator to the human tragedy around me.

And sometimes I am not just watching the ravens, I am one, flying over cities and countryside, over years and centuries. As I soar through the air, I feel the wind sliding over my shining feathers, and I feel completely, gloriously free.

I wake up one morning with the realization that this is the symbol I want for a tattoo. I've been intending to get one for a long time, but now I finally know what it should be. A raven.

Amazing that I haven't thought of it before, considering Carlo's nickname for me.

I surf the Internet, looking for the right picture.

I see ravens feeding on carcasses of rodents and small birds. No, thank you.

I see lots of perching ravens, big-beaked and fat and not so elegant.

And then I see it. The one I want.

It's a back view of a raven spreading its wings, its head turned to the side proudly. It's a raven whose wingspan has made it several times its size. It's a raven in position to take flight.

The tattoo will be black and white with a matte finish. I don't want any shine, any glam. Too bad I can't fly to L.A. to get Kat Von D to do it for me. She specializes in black and gray designs.

I can't believe I'm actually getting a tattoo.

It's a badass idea, and a bad-luck bird to boot.

In the past, I never could have done this alone. But here I am now, walking into the tattoo shop for my seven p.m. appointment to go under the needle.

Zaggy the tattoo artist is a walking work of art himself, with vines sprouting out of the neck and arms of his wife-beater. He's kind of scary-looking, but sweet and friendly, with a good reputation. He did the beautiful Chinese symbol on Kim's shoulder, and she told me that he was careful and sanitary, and he offers you breaks if the pain gets to you.

Zaggy takes me into the back. He tells me to take my shirt and bra off and lie on my front; he turns away while I do this. Across from me, a huge guy with a buzz cut is having an arm covered in Latin script. I don't know what it says, but I catch the word "Memoriam" and some dates in Roman numerals. A tribute to his fallen friends, I guess. We exchange a look, and he gives me an appreciative smile, and I'm suddenly conscious of the fact that I'm topless and he can probably see my left breast squashed against the table.

Zaggy places the stencil on my back and holds up a mirror so I can okay the placement.

"This your first tattoo?"

"Yeah. Is it gonna hurt like hell?"

"Nah. It'll bite, but this isn't one of the more sensitive places. Are you ready?"

"Uh, wait." I breathe in and out, trying to feel calm. "Yeah."

The needle descends, sears me like fire. "Owww."

He chuckles but doesn't stop. His left hand presses down on my back, holding me steady. "It takes some getting used to. We'll take a little break after I've done the outline."

Kim was right. Zaggy is cool. He asks questions that get me talking, thinking, taking my focus off the pain. About halfway through I have a mini panic attack—*What am I doing?*—but squelch it, telling myself that I can freak out later. There's no turning back now.

"We're done."

The words revive me. I let go of the table, my hands stiff from gripping it so hard. He angles the mirror so I can see my back.

Wow. It's just as I pictured it—even better.

The raven is here, proud.

I love it.

"Is this a bad time?" I ask from the office doorway. I've come to work an hour early, hoping we'd have the chance to talk.

"Not at all." Carlo gestures for me to have a seat.

"I've been curious about how it all began—the Jiang Shi, I mean."

"I wondered when you'd ask." He smiles. "It began with my sister. Daniella had been sickly since she was a little girl. Her illness dominated the life of my family for many years. You know how that is."

I sure as hell do.

"My family was obsessed with the mystery of her health. My father, a count in Florence, sent me to the university to study medicine. Looking back, the medical school caused far more harm than good. It was so primitive. We bled people for virtually any condition. We had no concept of how disease spread. I realized that the solution must be found elsewhere. I looked to philosophy, metaphysics, religion. I visited priests and bishops, many of whom promised me solutions through prayer. I paid them to pray for my sister. It never worked. My family's desperation only fed their greed."

"That's horrible."

"It was. A merchant friend of my father's spoke of an order of monks in the East that was rumored to have harnessed the soul's energy to cure disease. I traveled there, to the Jiangsu province of China, and heard legends of healing from villagers. They claimed that forty years before, the monks came down to the village to heal the sick, but after a few months, they abruptly stopped. No one could explain why, but the villagers said that anyone who had been healed did not age."

"Did you meet any of the people who didn't age?"

"Initially, no. The villagers refused to show me anyone who'd actually been healed by the monks. I sensed that the reason was fear. My intuition was confirmed when I was approached by an old woman who showed me a six-year-old boy she claimed to be her son. She demanded money before saying a word. She told me that a monk named Tolor had healed her son many years ago and that he'd returned soon after, saying that she must not reveal to anyone that her son had been healed. So she kept quiet and they eventually left the village for many years, returning only when she could claim he was her grandson. By the time she returned, none of the people who'd been healed remained in the village. She didn't know if they had been killed or if they'd fled. But she believed the monks had something to do with their disappearance."

"The monks scared them off?"

"That, or worse. I went to the monastery, pleading with the monks to show me a way to heal my sister. Most of them told me nothing, but one took pity on me; he said that even if they had found a way to heal using the power of the soul, to use it would be a grave mistake, because it would upset the cycle of life and death. The monks believed that death was part of the natural order of spiritual evolution. They saw it as God's will."

"But you had no problem upsetting the cycle, because you didn't believe in God."

"Right. The monk's warning only made me more determined to discover their secret. I also learned that the monk Tolor had left the monastery shortly after the healings had taken place." His black eyes gleam. "I found him."

"Was he a Jiang Shi?"

"No. He was an old man. I convinced him that I was worthy of the spell, that I could be trusted not to use it carelessly. He warned me, though, that the monks were becoming increasingly militant in tracking down those who'd been changed and killing them. Unfortunately, their mission lives on even today. They began the Order of the Heng Te."

"They're the scholar-warriors you talked about?" An uneasy feeling goes through me.

"Yes. Is this hard for you to hear, Raven?"

"I want to hear it. Go on with the story."

"At any rate, I returned home to Daniella, and her health was restored."

"And you decided to change yourself, too?"

"Yes. How could I pass up the opportunity? I had planned to do it in my thirty-fifth year, but when the plague came, it became necessary to do it sooner."

"What about your parents?"

"My father died in his sleep. I never had the chance to change him. And my mother, when she took ill, refused to be changed. She believed she'd be restored to health in the afterlife, and she was looking forward to it. She was confident that heaven was a much better place than earth and that she would see my father again. I could not take that away from her."

"Eventually you decided to change others besides your sister."

He nods. "As much as I enjoy my sister's company, I hoped that she would not be my only family for eternity. Over the years, I've had many opportunities to change people into Jiang Shi. Far too many opportunities, really. But I only allowed myself to change a few. I believe that the world is better off without the strife that would be caused by two kinds of human. All I wanted was to have a proper family—a group of people who could explore the world together, who'd be bonded by shared experience if not by blood. Humans have a great need to live within families."

He's right about that; it *is* what we want.

"There were practical reasons for keeping the group small too. Too many Jiang Shi would inevitably attract attention. If governments ever found out about my science, we would be lab rats. Right now, we are the stuff of legend."

"How did you decide who to make into Jiang Shi?"

"There was no particular method, but I chose people I admired. People of strength and resilience and character."

"Why did you choose Zin?"

His mouth crooks, as if he knows what I'm getting at. "Daniella's infatuation with him was the reason I considered him, but not the final reason I changed him. Zinadin is more than an entertainer, as you know. He brings a fire, a charisma, to everything he does. And he has an innate compassion and kindness that were rare in a young man of his day—of *any* day. Do you know why he took ill, Raven?"

"I guess there was a TB epidemic."

"Zinadin was traveling with the circus when he received word that a tuberculosis epidemic had hit his village and several of his family members were ill. He was strictly warned to stay away from the village until the epidemic passed. But he didn't."

I close my eyes. What a horrible choice to have to make—to be with your family and risk death, or to stay away and risk never seeing them again.

"He wasn't loved just for being an acrobat, Raven. He was loved for being the man he was."

"You sound proud of him."

"I am." The warmth in his eyes is unmistakable. I'll have to tell Zin about our conversation. He'll be glad to know Carlo feels that way.

"There is something I haven't told you, Raven. You may find it intriguing."

"What is it?"

"I dreamed you were coming to Evermore."

UNCERTAIN RUSTLING

"I'll have three Cosmos," I tell Zin a few minutes later.

"Cougars, huh?"

"You shouldn't judge people by their drinks."

"Am I wrong?"

I crack a smile. "No."

He smiles back, but it's a reserved smile. The kiss is still between us, as if it only happened last night.

As he makes the drinks, I try not to watch him, but don't succeed. I still wonder why he let that kiss happen in the first place. Was it a beginning for us, or just a slip of attraction? I'm afraid to ask. The truth is, no matter what was behind that kiss, he probably regrets it after the way I freaked out. He must think I'm immature. A typical immature mortal.

He is the brightest light I've ever known, and I am an idiot with a hole in my soul.

"Well?" he asks.

"Well what?"

"Aren't you going to deliver the drinks?"

"Oh."

I miss him. The intimacy we had. The endless phone conversations about everything and nothing. The silences in which we would just be.

I deliver the drinks, and the cougars don't even tip me. Oh well. I guess I took too long.

Before I can take another order, I notice that Zack, one of the part-timers, is manning the DJ booth.

"Where's Gabriel?" I ask Viola.

Her brows knit. "No one knows."

"Maybe he's stuck in traffic?"

"He usually has his cell with him. He should've been here an hour ago."

She looks worried, which makes me worried. Gabriel doesn't seem like the type to play hooky.

I go back to my customers. At some point I notice Carlo at the bar talking with Zin. I go up right after Carlo leaves. "Was that about Gabriel?"

Zin nods. "He left Carlo a note. We're having a meeting about it when we close. A Jiang Shi meeting."

"Can I go? I'm sort of . . . in on things."

"There's no need."

But Carlo disagrees. He finds me a few minutes later and tells me to go to the meeting. The tension is killing me. Why does everyone look so nervous?

After the club has closed and the part-timers have left, we gather in Carlo's office. "Gabriel is gone," he says. "He left me a note saying that he is leaving us for an indefinite period of time."

The room is dead silent. Carlo hands the note to Richard, who reads it, then passes it on. I read it last.

> Carlo,
> It is time I continue the next part of the journey on
> my own. I hope you and my beloved Jiang Shi will
> understand. Please let everyone know that I will miss
> them, and I expect to return one day.
> Gabriel

Mig bursts out, "What the hell is he thinking, going off on his own with the Heng Te out there?"

"I'm concerned for his safety also." Carlo's eyes skim over every one of us. "Does anyone know why he did this? Something must have led him to this decision."

Shrugs all around. Beside me, Zin is still. I can tell that Carlo is watching him.

Finally Zin speaks. "It's not that surprising. Gabriel was unhappy."

"I thought it was just a phase," Daniella says. "We all have our phases."

"I know his souls have been giving him trouble," Viola says. "Maybe it was too much for him."

Richard frowns. "Lately he's been talking about another Civil War. Maybe he wanted to be out of America in case it happens."

"Regardless of why he left, if he is in touch with any of you, please encourage him to come home." Carlo's voice is rough, and I know he's speaking from the heart. "We can't protect one another if we are not together."

"He'd better not have gone back to Uganda," Viola says.

I turn to Zin. "What about Uganda?"

"It was our last destination before we came here. Look, this is Jiang Shi business. It's nothing for you to worry about. I don't see why Carlo thinks you need to be here."

We look up to find Carlo's eyes on us. "She knows about us, so she should be here," he says.

Zin's eyes are defiant, but he says nothing.

"Wanna come over?" Zin asks after the meeting. "Order some pizza?" There's an urgency in his eyes that doesn't match his words.

"Sure."

We walk in silence. We haven't spent time just the two of us since the discovery of the hole in my soul, and I'm too nervous for small talk. I know this has something to do with Gabriel.

When the door is closed and locked, I ask, "What's going on?"

He plunks down on the couch, pulls me down next to him. "What I'm about to say will scare you, but I'm afraid I can't help it. It's time you know our suspicions."

"*Our* suspicions?"

"Gabriel's and mine." He takes a deep breath. "Carlo may want to hurt you."

"*What?*"

"I think he wants to make you a Jiang Shi."

"Why would he want that?"

"He likes you. Maybe he wants to add to the family. I've never seen him take this kind of interest in a mortal before. He acts like you're one of us."

"But that's because I know about all of you. I'm the only mortal who does, right? That's why he treats me the way he does."

"Gabriel and I think he hired Chris Harris. He might've planned to find you when you were dying and change you."

"That's crazy! Carlo would never do something like that."

"I know Chris Harris was stalking you that night, and I think he was hired to attack you. I have a vague sense of what he was thinking at the time. Sometimes I can tune in to his thoughts. . . . He was expecting money for his next hit, but not from you."

"I don't believe it."

"I don't want to believe it either. Neither does Gabriel. His suspicions go a lot further. He believes there's an afterlife. He thinks Carlo deceived us into thinking there isn't one so we'd continue to take souls."

"Is that what you think?"

"It's hard for me to believe that Carlo would deliberately lie to us. But I don't know. What scares me the most is that he seems to be fixated on you."

I want to deny it, but I can't. It would be a lie to say I didn't know that Carlo has some sort of special feeling toward me. He's been hinting at something ever since I got to Evermore. "Even if he's got this . . . fixation, that doesn't mean he'd want to hurt me."

"He might not see it as hurting you. And there's something else, Nic. Gabriel believes the Heng Te aren't real, that Carlo fabricated the myth centuries ago to scare us into banding together. To this day, Carlo is the only one who's ever encountered a Heng Te."

"What about the Jiang Shi who died?"

"Martine went missing. There was never a body. We have no proof of how she died except what Carlo told us. We all knew she'd been having trouble handling the souls inside her. One of them might have taken her over. Gabriel thinks Carlo could have used her disappearance as an opportunity to perpetuate the Heng Te threat."

None of this feels right. "You know where Gabriel is, don't you?"

He nods. "The Jiangsu province of eastern China. All the legends originate there. He thinks there might be a way to find out more about this science of the soul, as Carlo calls it. Gabriel has always resented Carlo for changing him into a Jiang Shi. He feels he was cheated out of finding out what lies beyond death. We decided that it's best to keep his mission a secret until there's evidence to confront Carlo, if he finds any."

"Can't you see into Carlo's soul? Wouldn't it tell you if he's been lying to you and if he's capable of hurting me?"

"Carlo's soul is opaque. It's like a wall of light—it's brilliant, but we can't see inside. He says it's because he prefers to keep his soul private, but he's never revealed to us how he was able to do it."

I remember Zin saying that you can know Carlo two hundred years and not know him at all. This must be why.

"Carlo called you Raven from the start. Did you ever wonder why?"

"The color of my hair."

"It's more than that. I snuck into his library. Ravens are mentioned in many of the old texts alongside the Jiang Shi. They're both seen as beings that cross between the realms of the living and the dead."

I get up, turn around, and lift the back of my shirt.

He blanches. "Carlo's suggestion?"

"No, he doesn't even know about it. Nobody does. I just wanted a tattoo, and I kept dreaming of ravens. It's true that I never thought about ravens before he starting calling me that, but—this is insane. I trust Carlo. I feel a connection between us."

His eyes narrow. "That could be his doing too. He's powerful. He made us all what we are. I don't know what else he can do. Look, I don't claim to be rational about this. After you got hurt that night, I felt this rage inside me. No one has the right to hurt you or change you. I won't lose you, Nic."

You don't have me, I almost say. But it would be a lie. He does have me, and he always will. Magnet and metal never change.

UNSEEN

I tell myself that the next time I set eyes on Carlo, I'll know. I'll know if he could possibly be behind the attack. I'll know if he's lying about the Heng Te.

I'll know if he's a master of deceit who tricked the Jiang Shi out of believing in an afterlife.

Before my shift starts, I approach him in the office. "Hey, Carlo."

"Raven." He puts his work aside. "How has your week been?"

So we talk about school and breakdancing, and the whole time I am thinking that my intuition should kick in and answer my question about Carlo, but nothing happens. Carlo is a locked box. His eyes give nothing away.

And neither, apparently, does his soul.

"I'd better get to work," I say, getting up.

"Is there something you wanted to ask me?"

"Ask you? No. Nothing."

"I thought you were working up to a question of some kind. No bother. Have a good shift."

"Thanks. See you later."

I leave the office, hip-hop sounds coming at me from all angles. What was I thinking? He obviously knew I was trying to figure him out. I just hope he doesn't suspect why.

How could I have no intuition at all about him? Isn't he the one who told me that intuition is everything?

"Kirk dumped me."

I jump. Viola has come up beside me.

"What happened?"

"He said I don't love him. That I don't take our relationship seriously. He was right. I never wanted to take it seriously, him being mortal and all. Most guys are cool with that. Most guys *like* that. But Kirk actually wanted something real."

"I'm sorry it didn't work out."

"Me too. He's a better guy than I ever realized."

"Are you going to try to get him back?"

"What's the point? I don't do long relationships with mortals anyway. None of us do. No offense, but dating mortals sucks."

"None taken."

"I won't say I'm not tempted to get back with him for a while. But he's better off if I let him go. I care about him enough to let him go."

She's right, no doubt.

She sighs. "Sometimes I tell myself it's time to be single and celibate for a while. But it never works. When I'm not in a relationship, I feel like I'm missing something. I'm always happier when I have that connection in my life. Friendship isn't enough. You know that yourself, don't you?"

I know that when it comes to me and Zin, friendship never seems like enough. But it's all I've got.

"I thought you and Zin would've gotten together a while ago, but that's Zin for you. He's always been the sensitive one. He can't do the whole loving and leaving thing like the rest of us. I worry about him."

"Why?"

"Because he loves you."

I blink. "Loves me?"

"Oh, right. I keep forgetting that you can't see his soul. Yes, he loves you. And you obviously love him. Your soul is as obvious about it as his."

My eyes widen. "So he *knows* that I love him?"

"Of course he knows. It's all over your soul. You might as well write it on your forehead."

"Oh God."

"Don't look so horrified. You both love each other, and you've got almost four years before he'll have to leave. That's a lifetime for a relationship for someone your age."

"What if four years isn't enough?"

She shrugs. "That's something you'll have to figure out. Um, Carlo's watching us. I think we should get out there."

I go up to some customers to take their order, then I approach the bar. My eyes take Zin in like I'm seeing him for the first time. Our gazes lock. I fall inside that green. Fall into him, like that first time I saw him dance.

He breaks the eye contact. "Got an order?"

I clear my throat. "Chocolate martini and a Strongbow."

"Gotcha." His eyes are still intense—as he drops them to do the drinks, I catch a flash of amber.

On my break, I head up to the balcony. I need to escape the crazy, to think.

I sit in the front pew, gazing down. I want to lose myself among those dancers, become one with them. Dancing is the closest I've ever come to losing myself. It's the closest I've been to getting high, the closest I'll ever be.

His footsteps startle me. As Zin approaches, his eyes pulsate like slow heartbeats. "You finally see."

"I thought you said Jiang Shi couldn't read minds."

"We can't. It was in your soul." He sits down next to me, touches my cheek. I close my eyes. "I still haven't scared you off, have I?"

"No."

"When I kissed you, I thought you were ready. I thought you wanted this. Then you saw into your soul and got so upset. I didn't want to push you."

"Why would you want to be with someone with a soul like mine? How can you even look past it? It's so awful."

"Everyone's soul has some damage. It's unavoidable. In mine, I still carry the loss of my family, two hundred years later."

"I'm sorry I freaked out on you."

"Don't be."

His hand slips to my neck, cradling it. He's going to kiss me. If I let him, there'll be no turning back.

Four years until he'll leave me. Four years, and I'll probably never set eyes on him again. Will I be strong enough to be with him and then let him go?

He gently turns my face to his, and I see his brilliant soul gleaming behind his eyes. I feel my soul quivering in my chest, rising. And I know there's no choice anymore, only destiny.

A voice breaks out of the darkness. *"Raven."*

We both jump. Carlo emerges from the shadows. "Your parents have been trying to reach you. Your brother is in the hospital."

DARKNESS

I am going to be the strong one, I tell myself as the night flits by my window. I'm going to carry them through this.

When we get to the ER, there's a lineup at reception, where a nurse is directing people. Seeing a sign that says INTENSIVE CARE, we head down a hallway, and then another hallway, and stop outside a door marked ICU.

A sign on the door directs us to a phone on the wall nearby. I pick it up and wait until I hear a voice on the line.

"My brother, Josh Burke, is in ICU. We'd like to see him."

A minute later a nurse opens the door. She is fiftysomething, with kind, motherly eyes. "The Burkes?" We all nod. She ushers us inside. "I'm glad we were able to get in touch with you. When Josh was brought in, he was in cardiac arrest."

I hear my mother's intake of breath.

"We were able to restart his heart, but I'm afraid he's now slipped into a coma."

The nurse pushes back the curtain, and we see him. He may be hooked up to a bunch of machines, but to me, he just looks like he's sleeping. He looks peaceful, more peaceful than I've seen him in so long.

My parents approach on either side of the bed and touch his hands. His face is flushed against the white sheets, maybe from the heat of the room. Mom leans forward and whispers something in his ear. I wonder if he can hear her.

I touch his matted hair, feel the warmth of his head under my hand. I realize that I'm not angry at him anymore, despite what he's done to himself, to my parents, to our family. What I feel for him is pure love.

We take off our coats. The nurse brings in an extra chair for my dad, and I sit on the edge of the bed. She closes the curtain when she leaves. Mom has silent tears on her cheeks, and Dad's face is anguished. It's hot and claustrophobic in here, like a tomb.

We don't move from his side, not for the bathroom, for coffee, for a break of any kind. We watch the fluctuating numbers on the monitor.

I open the curtain a few inches to let some air in. My parents exchange seats so that my dad is at the head of the bed, leaning over and holding Josh's hand.

"If he can just get through the night, maybe he'll be okay," Dad says.

"He'll be okay . . . whatever happens," I say. "I mean, even if . . . he'll be okay."

My parents look at me but don't say anything. They look back at their son.

Dawn breaks. A nurse suggests we might want to do shifts—two can go home to rest, another stay with him. None of us are willing to leave.

Around seven thirty, I offer to get them coffee and some food. They nod.

"While you're at it, could you call Emily?" Mom asks.

"Emily?" Josh's ex. His high school sweetheart.

Mom nods. "She'd want to know."

"Okay."

Mom hands me her cell, which has Emily's number programmed in.

I follow the arrows to the cafeteria. Before going in, I step aside and call Emily.

She answers. "Janet, is everything okay?"

"It's Nicole. We're at the hospital. Josh is in a coma." The words feel strange coming from my mouth. I wish I could swallow them back, make it not real.

"Oh my God. Which hospital?"

"New York Methodist."

"I'm coming right over."

"We're in ICU. You'd better tell them you're his fiancée. Only immediate family can come in."

"Okay. I'll be there soon."

I get in line for sandwiches. I check my watch, hoping I won't regret leaving the room.

Emily is number seven on Mom's contact list. I knew they were close when Emily was dating Josh through high school. I knew they still exchanged Christmas cards. I didn't realize they still talked.

Emily was always a calming influence on Josh. She even stayed with him through their first year of college, when his spiral began. I'm sure she put up with way more than she should have.

When they broke up, Josh told us she was an unsupportive, naggy, snobby bitch. We never believed it—we knew Emily. We felt ashamed, knowing how he must've treated her.

And still, Emily is on her way to the hospital.

I return to the room a few minutes later. Nothing has changed. My parents haven't moved.

Emily arrives just after nine o'clock. She and my mom hug. Emily has probably been more supportive of my mom through all of this than I have; in that one hug, I know it.

And I'm thankful.

I haven't seen Emily in more than a year. She's put on the freshman fifteen. I'm not used to seeing her in sweats and a mussed ponytail. She was always carefully put together.

She hugs my dad, then me.

"Thanks for coming," I say.

She frowns but says nothing. It hits me that she doesn't see this as being helpful. She feels she belongs here.

Positioning herself beside my mom, she puts an arm around her shoulders. My mom updates her on Josh's condition. Emily listens stoically, her eyes never leaving Josh's face.

Zin and I text back and forth:

JOSH IN HOSPITAL. WONT BE AT WORK TONIGHT. PLZ TELL CARLO.

WHICH HOSPITAL? ILL COME.

THANX BUT DONT COME. IM OK.

Shouldn't I want to run into his arms like I used to? But no, he doesn't belong here. He doesn't know Josh, and he isn't close to my family. It wouldn't feel right to bring him here, not now.

Josh never moves except the slight rise and fall of his chest. His eyes don't even move beneath his lids to indicate he's dreaming. His vitals occasionally dip, then stabilize. We can see and hear every heartbeat, every falter, on the machine. I'm focused on the beats, willing the next one to come. I hold his hand as if my touch keeps him alive.

One day blends into another, with no beginning and no end. We do shifts, with one or two of us going home to sleep for a few hours. Since I'm used to staying up all night, I stay during the darkest hours while my parents go home, and then I get some sleep in the morning.

On the fifth day, the news comes.

His brain function is nonexistent. The doctors want us to consider taking him off life support.

Tears blur the sight of my family collapsing.

He's already gone. He slipped through our fingers while his heart kept beating.

My mind is transported to two summers ago, our family trip to the Grand Canyon. We've stopped at Yavapai Point to watch the sunset. Mom and Dad stay close to the car, while Josh and I trek out a little ways to a point where there is no guardrail, and the canyon is surrounding us. I stay several feet back from the edge, while Josh walks up to it, and I have a sudden fear that a gust of wind might carry him away.

"Josh."

He takes a step back, with a sheepish smile. I don't think he wanted to be that close to the edge either.

We look out at the canyon's breathtaking hugeness. All the anxiety I carry within me seems to melt away. School, drama, grades—none of it matters anymore. It's just me and the canyon and the orange sun and my brother beside me. A blissful stillness washes over me.

"Gives perspective," I say.

"Yeah."

We're silent for a long time. The sun is mostly behind the mountains now. The colors go from sand to faded grays and dusky reds.

I close my eyes and listen to the wind whipping against rocks. I don't think I've ever really heard the wind before.

I sigh, opening my eyes. "Makes you look inside yourself. It's soothing." I turn to Josh, whose eyes are fixed on some distant point.

"Did you ever look inside yourself and see . . . nothing?" he asks.

"No. Did you?"

He nods. "I tried meditating a few times. I thought it could help me still my mind. Sometimes my mind just won't stop. . . . I didn't like where it took me."

"What do you mean?"

"I don't know. Something in me just felt . . . empty. Like there was no purpose, no point to anything. Like there was no *me*." He's looking at me now, searching my face for understanding.

"Well, maybe you just didn't go deep enough."

"But what if that's who I am?"

"You're not empty, deep down. No one is."

He doesn't look convinced. He turns back to face the canyon, swathed in the fading gray of dusk.

My parents won't even talk about disconnecting Josh's life support. Not yet. But they can't avoid the question for much longer.

We know he's already gone. But the idea of disconnecting him, the finality of it, is unbearable. It would mean he was gone forever.

The clock reads 8:37 p.m. I'm not sure what day it is. Emily and I walk the halls. Every footstep feels heavy, like walking through snowdrifts.

"Thanks for being there for my mom."

"She was there for me, too." Emily tries to smile. "She told me about your dancing, that you're part of a breaker group. That's awesome."

"Thanks. You should stop by Evermore some Friday or Saturday night. Sometimes we battle other groups." I try to think of something else to say. "How's college?"

"Stressful, but good. I can't believe I'm almost half done with my undergrad. Have you chosen a college yet?"

"No."

"Did you apply to Columbia?"

"Not my thing, even if I could get in."

She looks surprised. "Well, it's a great school and it means you can stay close to home—um, if that appeals to you."

She obviously knows that I've been doing everything possible *not* to stay close to home this past year. But there's no judgment in her eyes. "You're an amazing person, Nic. Your mom told me about what happened to you recently. She said that when you were in the hospital, you were the one who helped them keep it together. You've been the same way these past few days. In fact, you've always been that way, ever since I've known you."

I'm not sure what to say to that. It's the opposite of how I feel. The only reason I'm calm is because I don't want my parents to worry about me. I'm a train wreck inside. Whenever I look at Josh, it hurts so much I could scream.

"Even when you were really young, you knew who you were," she says. "Life didn't intimidate you. You took things as they came. Josh was never like that."

"I wasn't as easygoing as all that, but next to Josh, who stressed over every little thing, it must've looked that way. He was always such a perfectionist. He couldn't handle being anything less than the best. I think it's part of what drove him to . . . you know."

"I know. Remember the time he placed second at the state Math Olympics? To him, it was a total failure. He put on a good front, but he was so insecure. I tried to help him. He never listened."

"You helped him a lot. He'd have gone off the rails a lot sooner if it weren't for you."

She sighs. "I don't know about that. When things started to get really bad, I bailed. I just couldn't take it. He could be so angry sometimes. But I keep thinking that if I'd hung on a little longer, he wouldn't have gotten so self-destructive."

"You can't think like that. You stuck by him longer than most people would have."

She presses a tissue against her eyes. "I tried. I just wish . . ."

"You did everything you could. At some point you had to save yourself from him. We all look back and wonder if we should've done something differently. But there's no point."

The despair on her face is a mirror of my own. "I thought it would work out somehow," she says. "I thought he'd eventually go to rehab, get better, and we'd pick up where we left off."

"We all hoped he'd give rehab a go. Whenever any of us tried to talk to him, it would end up a shouting match. By the end, he hated me." The gravity of it hits me. My brother will die hating me. My last memory of him will be of his angry taunts that night at Evermore. I feel sick.

"He loved you, Nic."

"A long time ago, maybe."

"Not so long ago. Even when we were starting college, he'd

sometimes brag to me about the wise things you'd come up with. Like you were the oracle of knowledge."

"Seriously?"

She nods. "He had a lot of respect for you."

The tattoo on my back prickles. I look up. Carlo is standing at the end of the hall.

"Can I meet you back at the room? I'll be along in a couple of minutes."

"Sure." She heads back the other way.

Carlo and I approach each other. His black eyes are grave. When his arms encircle me, I fall against him.

"Zin told me what's happened. He said your brother is on life support and the doctor has advised that it be disconnected."

I nod, taking a step back. "My parents don't want to remove it yet. I don't know how long—" And then all the tears I've been holding back come out in a flood.

"Shh . . . I want to help." His voice is so soft that I can barely hear him above my sobs.

"There's n-nothing you can do. His brain function is gone. Once it's gone, you c-can't get it back."

"Your brother's life does not have to end."

My mind kicks in. I step away from him. "Don't say it. Please. It's not an option."

"I know the concept of immortality is difficult for you."

"It's wrong. Taking souls . . . it's almost like murder."

"Man has always survived by putting his own survival before that of others. Don't forget, we take only the souls of people who are near death. Do you feel we're all murderers? Is that how you see us?"

"I didn't mean that. But I still don't want my brother to be . . ."

"You prefer that he dies?"

"I don't want him to die! But if it happens, his soul will live on. He'll be with God."

"I urge you not to let your reservations deny your brother another chance at life. I can give you the old Josh back. The one who was kind."

The one who was kind. He knows how much I want the old Josh back. So much it's tearing me up inside. But at what cost? If I give in, would Josh thank me or hate me?

"Why do you care about my brother?"

"I care about you. That's why I'm here."

His black eyes take hold of me, and I know it's true. He cares about me. He knows I love Josh. He knows I'd do almost anything to bring him back.

But what right do I have to sentence Josh to eternity on earth, to survival by taking souls? I can't. I won't. I won't be responsible for altering the destiny Josh created for himself. Who am I? I'm not God.

Neither is Carlo.

"Thank you for the offer, Carlo. But my answer is no."

Before he can say anything, I turn away and head back to the room. I expect him to follow me, to keep trying to change my mind. And maybe I want him to. But when I look back over my shoulder, he's gone.

I return to the ICU, entering quietly so as not to disturb anyone. Through the curtain, I see Emily alone with Josh. She is whispering to him, pressing his hand over her heart. Before she can see me, I slip out of the room. She deserves to have a few minutes alone with him to say whatever she needs to say.

I find my parents in the lounge next to the cafeteria. There's a TV hanging from the wall, tuned to CNN. I squeeze in between them on the couch and curl up. I feel their arms around me.

A few minutes later we get up on shaky limbs. Mom and I head back to the ICU, and Dad goes into the bathroom.

Mom and I walk in—and stare.

Josh is sitting up in bed, his arms around Emily. His blue eyes land on us. "Mom, Nic, join the hug!"

BLESSED

I'm too shocked to move.

Mom rushes into Josh's arms. "Oh, honey, we thought we'd lost you! It's a miracle!"

But it's not a miracle.

It's Carlo.

I fly to Josh, and we hold him tight, a circle of love. *This can't be happening,* I keep thinking. But it *is* happening. Josh is back.

"You'll never lose me, Mom." He kisses the top of her head. "You look like you've had a rough time these past few days. Em was just telling me it's been touch and go."

Mom nods, too choked up to speak. She clings to him. I pull back, wiping my eyes. Josh reaches out and grabs my hand. "I missed you, Nic."

"Me too."

My dad walks in, stops dead. Then he rushes over, throwing his arms around his son. A nurse stands there, dumb-founded, before hurrying out.

We all stand around Josh, hugging and crying.

"You're alive," Dad keeps saying. I've never seen such joy on his face, never.

"He healed me," Josh says.

"Who?" my parents ask.

"I don't know. I woke up and he was right there, checking that my vital signs were okay. It's like he was a doctor . . . but he was wearing a suit." He looks at Emily, who's wiping her tears with a wad of tissue.

"I don't know who he was," she says. "A faith healer, I guess. He told me to put my hands on his head. He put his hands over mine. Spoke in some language. There was this light. It went through us. . . ."

The doctor comes in, eyes wide behind his glasses. "This is incredible."

"Wouldn't be the first time they called me incredible," Josh says. "So, can I go home now?"

"Uh, no, definitely not. I'd like to do some more tests, make sure you've completely stabilized."

We step out of the way so the doctor can approach Josh. He checks his pulse and blood pressure manually, amazement written all over his face. Then he examines the machines, as if there might have been a malfunction.

He's not going to find the logical explanation he's looking for.

Josh sits through this for a few minutes, then looks plaintively at the IV. "Can I get some real food?"

I wake up the next day just after one in the afternoon. Thankfully Mom and Dad didn't wake me for school. They couldn't have reasonably expected me to go after the exhaustion of the last few days.

I hurry downstairs to find a note on the kitchen table.

> *Hey, sleepyhead! We'll be at the hospital visiting Josh until three o'clock. There are also visiting hours from six to eight if you want to stop by then. We'll bring a pizza home for dinner. Love, Ma and Pop*

I exhale. It wasn't a dream. Josh is okay.

If being a Jiang Shi is okay.

Carlo. I want to hug him. I want to slap him. I don't know what I want, or what I should feel.

Josh is alive. Alive *and well.*

A feeling rushes through me. Joy.

I call Zin.

"It's good to hear your voice, Nic. How is he?"

"He's great."

"Great?" He sounds surprised. Then I remember that my last

text said we were considering taking Josh off life support.

"He was close to death, but then Carlo showed up."

There's a long silence.

"Zin, are you there?"

"You're telling me he changed Josh."

"Yeah. You should've seen Josh yesterday. He was so alert and happy. He was even cracking jokes."

"That's good to hear." But his voice is restrained.

"What is it?"

"Nothing. I know how much you love him. I can't blame you for doing what you did."

"It wasn't my choice. I told Carlo not to change him, but he went ahead and did it anyway."

"You're serious."

"Yeah." Tears fill my eyes. "Josh would be dead right now if Carlo had listened to me."

"It took a lot of strength to say no."

"How could letting my brother die be the right thing? I'm glad Carlo didn't listen to me."

"You believe in an afterlife. So do most people. There's no reason you should feel guilty."

"Josh is different now. We have him back, really back, the way he used to be."

"That's wonderful, Nic."

But his voice isn't convincing. I can tell he thinks changing

Josh was a bad idea. "You don't sound like it's wonderful."

"Just give me some time to wrap my brain around this. Carlo hasn't changed anyone in two hundred years, and he only changes . . . certain types of people."

"What's that supposed to mean? Josh isn't good enough to be a Jiang Shi?"

"I'm not saying that. But you know as well as I do that Carlo carefully chose everyone he's changed. He never changed anyone who wasn't mentally well before."

"Josh can handle being a Jiang Shi. You'll see."

"I hope you're right. We won't know for sure until he takes his first soul. But that won't be for a long time."

A long time. When I'll be long dead.

When I arrive at the hospital, Josh is sitting up. His scraggly goatee is gone—and so are the sunken cheeks, the purple shadows under his eyes, the scabs on his skin.

He looks young and fresh-faced. Healthy.

But the most startling difference is his eyes. They're clear and with-it, and they light up when I walk into the room. "Hey, Nic! I was hoping you'd stop by."

I hug him, then sit on a chair by the bed. "How are you feeling?"

"Like I should be running a marathon, not cooped up in this room."

"You look good. When can you come home?"

"Doc says tomorrow, if all the tests come up okay. He's just stalling because he can't explain my turnaround. He doesn't believe that a faith healer was here. It's still hard for *me* to believe. But this man, whoever he was, saved my life. I have to find him and thank him. And I want to ask how in God's name he pulled it off. Do you believe in angels?"

"I don't know."

"Me neither. I just keep thinking, why did he choose me? Why have I been given this second chance when so many other people, so many good people, die?"

"You're a good person, Josh. You always have been. It's just that . . . you got addicted and everything went downhill. It doesn't change who you are."

"I remember *him*, the way he thinks. He didn't deserve a miracle."

"Josh, you were an addict. It's a disease. You can't blame yourself." But my words don't feel true. I blamed him for destroying himself, for destroying our family. Who else could I blame?

"You don't need to say that, Nic. I made my choices. I'll make different ones this time." He gives me a reassuring smile. "When God gives you a chance like this one, you can't waste it."

Soon he'll know the truth about why he's still alive. Carlo is going to crush his idea of God.

DAYS OF YORE

It's sheer cruelty that I'm expected to go to school the next day. I want to be at the hospital with my parents when Josh gets discharged. I want to keep pinching him, and myself, to be sure it's real.

There's no chance of relapse now. No chance of disaster. There's not even a chance that some random accident will steal his life away. I can actually sit in class and think about Josh and not have a tense, ominous feeling in my stomach.

I feel lighter, so much lighter that I bet Zin will notice it in my soul.

Couldn't Zin just be happy for me? I'm surprised that he, of all people, is questioning Carlo's judgment when he's only alive because of it.

At lunch my friends are hesitant to ask questions. They know the reason why I was MIA for a few days—I gave Zin permission to tell them about Josh's overdose.

I decide to come clean. Officially. "He's had a problem for a while. I'm sorry I didn't tell you guys."

"You didn't need to tell us anything," Slide says. "It's a family thing."

Chen slaps me on the back. "Yeah. We all got family things. He gonna be okay? He can't fall back into the coma, can he?"

"No. He's being released from the hospital today."

"Must've been a hellish few days," Slide says. "Guess you won't be up for Hip-Hop 'n Bowl tonight."

"Yeah, I'd better stay in. Some family time is called for."

"We're so glad he's okay," Kim says. "Have you talked to him about rehab? Or maybe it's too early, if he's just being released today."

"I'm sure my parents will talk to him about it." *Though he won't need it*, I don't say. "I have a feeling that this experience has woken him up. I think he'll turn around. And it'll be for real this time."

My friends are nodding, but I bet they're skeptical. I don't blame them. I would be too.

They don't know what I know.

When I get home, Mom is in the kitchen cooking mac and cheese, Josh's favorite.

"Yum." I hug her. "Where is he?"

"In his room."

I run upstairs. It's surreal, seeing Josh in his old bedroom. He's sitting on his bed, tearing his old posters into strips. His walls used to be plastered with heavy metal posters, and now they're completely bare.

He looks up. "Do you think I can recycle these? I'm not sure if you can recycle paper with a glossy finish."

"I'm not sure either." I plunk down on his bed. "Redecorating, I see."

"I'll be happier without these all around me." He tears another poster, right through Marilyn Manson's demonic eye. "I'm fine with the walls being bare right now. I'll paint it white. I hate this navy."

"Me too. It's not you anymore."

"It was never me. I don't know who the hell that other guy was . . . I just hope I never meet him again."

I can see the flicker of doubt in his eyes, the fear that he'll slide again. He has no idea that he can't become an addict, because Jiang Shi are immune to disease.

"You'll have to get used to sharing a bathroom again," he says.

"Damn." I grin, remembering how we use to fight over it. He was always the one who took forever. I'd accuse him of being prissier than a girl. Come to think of it, he wasn't any worse than Rambo.

"How was school?" he asks.

"Blah."

"You're graduating in a couple months. That's pretty cool."

"I guess so."

"Your enthusiasm is contagious. Mom says she doesn't know your plans for next year. She's afraid to ask you about it."

"I got into a few places, but I know there isn't money. Maybe I'll go to City College . . . or maybe I'll take some time off."

"I know it's my fault there's no money. I don't know what to say. Sorry doesn't seem like enough."

"Don't worry about it. I'm just happy you're well."

"Thanks. If you do end up going to City College, we'll probably be on campus together. Hope that doesn't cramp your style. I called a few minutes ago and an adviser said that with my SAT scores I should have no problem getting in."

"You've decided this already?"

"I figured it all out last night. The only way I'm going to be able to pay Mom and Dad back before they retire is if I get a high-paying job. That means going back to college right away. We can't afford Columbia anymore, so I'll go to City College. If my marks are as good as I think they'll be, I'll be able to get into a decent law school."

"Wow. You've planned out your future in less than twenty-four hours, and I'm still confused about what to do next year."

"You know I always intended to go to law school. If I hadn't screwed up, I'd be halfway through my BA by now. But I'll catch up. That's what night and summer classes are for. I was thinking I'll spend my early career in corporate law, then later, once I'm set financially and I've paid Mom and Dad back, I'll move into human rights law and legal aid."

"That's quite the plan."

Same old Josh, planning and obsessing. I guess that part doesn't change when you become immortal—your personality stays the same. Still, he shouldn't be able to drive himself over the edge this time. Not when there's no edge for him to go off.

I am at the dinner table with my family. We're chatting, laughing. It's as if we've reverted back to the old days, the days of potential.

Josh still drowns his mac and cheese in ketchup. I still tell him it's pointless, because you can't taste the cheesiness. He still doesn't listen.

My parents are on a high. They're smiling so much they can hardly keep the food in their mouths.

"Emily's coming over at eight," Josh says. "She's bringing a movie and Jiffy Pop. You guys up for it?"

"Sure," Dad and I say at once.

Mom nods. "Sounds good!"

Is this my family?

Dessert is Josh's favorite flavor of Ben & Jerry's, Chunky Monkey. Josh has three huge scoops. He's been eating like he hasn't seen food in decades. There's no question he's a Jiang Shi.

"You'll have some weight on in no time," Mom says.

"I hope to gain twenty pounds by September."

"That would be a fun goal to have." Mom laughs. "Some of us need to go in the opposite direction."

It's good to see that Mom can laugh about it. She must have gained twenty pounds over the last couple of years, and I know it's because of her worries about Josh. But now that Josh's back, she can focus on getting healthy again.

Josh grins. "Yeah, there are worse things than putting on weight, but I'm going to do it right. I'll eat healthy and go to the gym. You go to the Y, huh, Nic? It's decent?"

"And cheap. I have a few guest passes I can give you."

"Great."

"Just be careful not to put too much strain on your body too quickly," Dad says.

"I will."

After dinner Josh gathers the plates and starts washing the dishes. My parents look at each other. Even when he was well, Josh never helped out.

Josh laughs. "What are you staring at? Since you're not charging me rent, I'm going to pull my weight around here. Nic, you wanna dry?"

Emily shows up just before eight, and we start watching the movie. It's a Will Ferrell comedy that cracks us up from the first scene. I can't remember the last time I hung out with my family.

For the first time in a long time, I don't want to be anywhere but here.

Around eleven thirty p.m. my phone lights up. I was hoping it would.

"You weren't sleeping, were you?"

It's just a formality; Zin knows I'm never in bed before midnight. "No. You on break?" I can hear the street behind him.

"Yeah. I wanted to find out how things are going."

I picture him outside Evermore, without a coat despite the chilly night, and I can almost catch the scent of him. "It's been great. We had a family dinner just like old times. You should've seen him eat. He's worse than you."

He chuckles. "He's got some catching up to do."

"Yeah. And get this, he's already planning for the fall. He wants to go back to college."

"You always said he was driven."

"Definitely. I was thinking . . . what about you telling him that he's a Jiang Shi? Maybe it would seem less scary coming from you."

"It should really be Carlo. He changed him, and he knows why. He can make sense of the Jiang Shi existence better than any of us can, especially me."

Maybe he's right. Zin, with his suspicions about Carlo, might confuse Josh.

"Have you heard from Gabriel?" I ask.

"Not yet."

I take a breath. "I hope he finds the answers soon."

"Me too. I want to trust Carlo. But I mostly want to know the truth. And listen, I'm sorry I didn't react the way you hoped to Josh being changed. I guess I wasn't ready for there to be another Jiang Shi."

"It's okay. You know I was against it at first. But now that I have him back, I can't question it. I love him too much to wish it hadn't happened."

"You're an angel, Nic," he says softly.

"Thanks. Actually, Josh thought Carlo might have been an angel."

Zin laughs. "Now *that's* funny. I'd have thought an angel is the last thing Carlo would be mistaken for."

"I can see it, though. He's so dark, but there's something ethereal about him."

"Ethereal? You sound like you have a crush on him."

I laugh, and he does too. Jealousy could only ever be a game between us, because he knows my soul. And he knows there's no one but him.

"So you're coming in to work tomorrow night, right?" he asks.

"Yeah."

"Feels like I haven't seen you in years." He pauses, and I know he's thinking of our last moment together on the balcony. "I really wanted to call you earlier, see if you wanted to get together . . . but I knew you'd want to spend time with your family."

"Yeah. I even passed on Hip-Hop 'n Bowl."

"That says something. Rambo's still going on about his new bowling shoes. I just don't get it."

"Me neither."

"Well, I've got to get back. But I'll see you tomorrow night. I've missed you, Nic."

"I've missed you, too."

INTO THE TEMPEST

The next night I get to work half an hour early. The office door is open.

Carlo is at his desk when I walk in, bathed in the glow of candlelight. He gets up, comes around his desk. "Raven." He gives me a long look. "Should I apologize?"

"No."

He smiles. "Good. I only did what you wanted me to, but were afraid to sanction. I saw the truth in your soul."

"I know. Thank you."

"Have a seat," he says, and returns to his chair.

"I . . . can't explain how much you've done for my family. It means everything that Josh is okay." I am determined not to cry. There are things we need to talk about. Important things. "Josh thinks you're a faith healer or an angel. He wants to thank you. When are you going to tell him the truth?"

"I wanted to ask you that question. Normally I wait several

weeks until the person has gotten their bearings. What do you think?"

"I think you should tell him right away. I can tell he's worried that he could become an addict again, and I don't want him to have to deal with that. Plus, he's already making plans to go to college in the fall. And he's on his way to getting back together with his ex-girlfriend. I just think he needs to know the truth."

"I'll tell him tomorrow. You can give him my number and we can arrange to meet."

"Okay." I can't help but feel nervous. Josh is going to know the truth. He's going to find out that he can't settle in one place for more than ten years at a time. That he'll be expected to go to war-torn areas of the world with the others. He'll know that all of this happened because of my connection to Carlo. And he might hate me for it.

"I wouldn't worry, Raven. Most people like the idea of being immortal."

"Josh has never been like most people."

"What about you? Would you like to be immortal?"

My heart skips a beat. I think of Zin and Gabriel's suspicions about the attack. But I still can't believe it's true. "I guess the answer is . . . sometimes."

He raises his brows. "Even after your brother has been changed? You wouldn't want to join him?"

"What does it matter if I want to join him or not? I'm not dying."

"No, you are not. I thought, however, that you may have had the dreams."

"What dreams?"

"Of the raven."

My throat feels dry. "I've had some weird dreams."

"I think it is time you know what your destiny is, Raven. I envisioned it many decades ago." His stare is so intense, I almost forget to breathe. "I knew that when the raven appeared, a raven with a teardrop in her eye, the new era of the Jiang Shi was near."

He walks toward me. He's so close that my pulse is wonky, as if he has an electromagnetic field around him. Then he places a hand on my back, right over the tattoo. *He knows.* I've covered the tattoo so well, but he knows.

"I had hoped you would come to the realization yourself, but I don't feel I can wait any longer. You are destined to be one of us, Raven."

"One of you? Meaning . . ."

"Yes. It is your destiny to become a Jiang Shi."

I'm speechless. I look at him, hoping his serious expression will crack into a smile. But as he once said, humor isn't his forte.

"It may be hard to accept, but I have foreseen it. In six hundred years, I have never had a vision that has not come true."

"I'm sorry, Carlo, but I don't see this happening."

"It doesn't matter if you can envision it or not. It's what is that matters. I hope that you will take my advice and consent to be changed into one of us. If you leave it up to fate, it may be more painful."

I swallow. "What are you asking me to do?"

"You must submit to a controlled overdose, a pharmacological cocktail that will put you into cardiac arrest. I will be right there with you, ready for the moment when you can be changed. The only way to become a Jiang Shi is to be at the point of death, when one's soul loosens its hold on the body, ready to abandon it."

"This is crazy. You could miss the moment and my heart could stop."

"That would be highly unlikely. The heart will struggle before it fails. That is the window in which I will act. However, I will have a defibrillator at hand, just in case."

"You think I'd let myself be poisoned?"

"As I said, if we don't do it ourselves, fate will find its way, and it will likely cause you worse suffering than what I am proposing."

"You expect me to jump at this?"

"Not jump, perhaps, but consider."

"I can't believe this." I press my fingers to my temples. "This is insanity."

"So many shifting paradigms in such a short time for you, Raven. It's natural to feel the way you do."

I look into his black eyes. Angel or devil?

My eyes drop. I can't look at him anymore. Why should I? He sees everything anyway.

"You love our Zinadin. And he loves you. There is only one thing standing between you."

My mortality.

I stagger out of Carlo's office like I'm drunk.

It's unreal. I have just been given the chance to be with Zin forever. To never get old, never die. To explore the far reaches of the world. Everything a person could ever dream of.

Part of me wishes he hadn't given me a choice. If something were to happen to me and he made me a Jiang Shi—fine. But no one except Carlo has ever chosen to become a Jiang Shi.

What am I really giving up by saying no to mortality? The answers come back in a flood: a normal life, career, kids, stability.

Everything I know and expect out of my life.

And the chance to find out what lies beyond. The chance to find out if there's really a light.

Weird, but I always expected I'd have kids one day. I don't know why. You can raise them right and they can still get screwed up. And when they get screwed up, it can ruin your life. You'll never be happy again. Why would anyone sign up for that?

"Spaced out, huh?" Zin leans his elbows on the bar.

"Yeah."

"Good to see you."

"Same here."

"What did Carlo say about telling Josh?"

"Um, tomorrow. He'll tell him tomorrow."

"Is something wrong?"

"No." Maybe I'm not lying. I don't know if something's wrong or not. All I know is, I have to think this through myself. Zin will freak out if I tell him about Carlo's offer. Or will he?

I look around. "I should take some orders."

"Okay. By the way, the Toprocks are coming tonight." He places a hand over mine, and a kick of electricity goes through me. "We'll dance later."

I nod, then search for customers. He's never said it that way before. *We'll dance later.*

We'll dance forever if . . .

I can't let my thoughts take this direction. If I choose to become a Jiang Shi, it shouldn't be about Zin.

According to Carlo, I have no say whether I become a Jiang Shi or not, I only have a say as to when and how it happens. But Carlo could be wrong. Zin and Gabriel think he might be wrong about the afterlife. Why not about his vision?

I should only do this if it's what I really want to do.

The Toprocks and Kim show up around midnight. They're

pumped, heading immediately to the dance floor. I take a break to dance with them.

Kim's usual hand flurries are accented by a new shoulder roll. Slide points at her. "You've been workin' on that!"

"It's just a move, Slidey. I've got more where that came from."

"Whoa," we all say.

"My girl could be a breaker one day, who knows?" Chen grins.

"It's my greatest dream, Chenny Wenny."

"I've got it," Rambo says. "We'll train her so she can join the Spinheads and screw up all their battles!"

Kim flicks her blue bangs. "I'd be happy to, Bo. While I'm at it, I'll tell all the girls in the bar that you're wearing bowling shoes."

"Go ahead. Who could blame me? Who else has shoes that can slide like this?" He demos a few moves, gliding on slippery soles.

"I'm impressed," I have to say.

"Me too. I should get a pair." Zin's on the floor beside me. "You should've told me you were going on break."

"Sorry."

I am so full of angst, I have to let loose. My eyes drift mostly closed, and I let the music take me over. I can faintly see my friends moving their bodies to beats that trickle like rain. Dry ice settles in the air, turning the dance floor into an icy dream.

My eyes are drawn to Zin, whose moves are fluid in the mist. I remember the first time I saw him, his light burning through the fog.

The mist thickens. We're almost blind and nearly choking on its dry sweetness, but we'll never stop dancing. A feeling of claustrophobia comes over me as I wonder if the mist will ever lift, if we're all trapped. Then I feel strong arms around my waist and Zin's face close to mine, as if to say, *It's just us now.*

His lips brush my cheek, and his body is moving with mine. He's caught on to my rhythm, and his hands are pressed to the small of my back, keeping me close. Green eyes hover in front of me with a question still waiting to be answered.

Do you want this?

I put a hand behind his head and bring his face close to mine. Brushing my lips against his, our mouths meet. Heat pours over us like honey, and we move as one, the way we were meant to.

There is only one thing standing between you. The voice in my head is Carlo's. And at this moment, there's only one possible answer.

Yes. Now. Forever.

Zin must've sensed the intrusion of thought, because he pulls back, his hands touching the sides of my neck. The mist around us is beginning to dissolve, and the forms start taking the shapes of people, reminding us that we're not alone. "Will you come over later?" he asks.

I have a decision to make. A decision from which there's no turning back. And I have to make it myself. If I don't, I could regret it, and blame him forever.

"Not tonight. I need . . . to think. But I will tomorrow. I promise."

He smiles. "Then tomorrow it is."

When I get into bed that night, I tell myself that I will wake up with an answer. My dreams will explore my dilemma using a bunch of symbols that I will neatly unravel in the morning. And my decision will be obvious.

But my subconscious doesn't care about my dilemma, because in my dreams, I'm lying with Zin amid white sheets. Our bodies are so close I can feel his breath against my lips. We are kissing deeply, and there is no rush. It's as if we've been transported outside of time.

He smoothes my hair back from my face, pressing his lips to my cheek, to my temple. I glimpse his face, the love glistening in his eyes.

His lips skim down my neck, speaking softly in an old melodic language I can't identify. But I feel what he's saying.

I realize that we're naked, and it doesn't seem strange at all. It's natural, joyous, like we were meant to be together this way.

My hands splay on his chest, feeling the warmth of his skin, the beat of his heart. I slide my hands over his abs, and I hear him suck in a breath, then laugh. Zin's laugh fills me with bliss. I'm laughing too.

He kisses my body reverently, each touch of lips to skin igniting me. I look down at his black hair, watch him tease my belly button. He looks up at me, his eyes flashing like a rapid heartbeat, his lips parted hungrily.

And then he slides over me, and we are one.

I wake up in a tangle of covers and lust.

So much for finding answers in my sleep.

I head downstairs to find Josh in the kitchen with my parents, drinking coffee in their pajamas.

"Something smells good." I turn to the stove. "French toast!"

"I'm making enough for you, too," Josh says.

"Awesomeness." In what universe does Josh make us breakfast?

In a universe where the Jiang Shi have eternal life, comes the answer.

A tremor goes through me at the thought that today Josh will find out the truth. I will slip him Carlo's number, then leave it to Carlo to fill in the rest.

Josh has never been good at accepting change of any kind. He's always been about routine, control. Now he'll be told something that will change his entire view of his life and the world.

How's he going to deal?

I'm glancing out my bedroom window. The late afternoon sun is fading behind a mass of cloud. Josh has been gone for four hours already.

I've spent most of the day lounging around the house, staring out windows, swimming in thought. I'm no closer to having an answer for Carlo, or for myself. I can't seem to separate the decision to become a Jiang Shi from my love for Zin, and until I can do that, I feel I'm not deciding for the right reason.

Is love a reason to choose immortality? How can I know Zin will love me forever? Will it last fifty years, or a hundred, and then I'll spend eternity alone?

I'm jolted back to the present when I spot Josh getting out of the car. Hurrying downstairs, I throw open the front door before he can unlock it. "How'd it go?"

He steps in, looks around. "Mom and Dad home?"

"No."

His lips spread in a smile. "I can't believe you knew this whole time!"

"Yeah, well."

He goes into the kitchen, hoists himself onto the counter. "I'm almost afraid to believe it, you know? Carlo made me prove it to myself. All I had to do was look in the mirror, see into my own soul. And it hit me that since I woke up, I've been seeing into people's souls, I just didn't know it." He gives me a penetrating look. "Carlo was right. Your soul is brilliant."

"You can see it from over there?"

"Yeah. It's amazing. And perfectly whole. Not like most."

Oh my God. *The hole is gone.*

He's right, I can feel it. Since he woke up in the hospital, since I've had my family back, the hole is gone.

It feels wonderful.

And yet it feels like cheating. Didn't Zin say we all carry loss in our souls? Why shouldn't I have to, like everyone else?

I shouldn't question it. I should just thank God for it.

Or Carlo.

"Immortality, Nic. Can you believe it? Age can't touch me. Neither can sickness. Do you know what that means? I'll never be an addict again."

I smile. "I know."

"When Carlo said that a Jiang Shi can never be an addict, it was like I was let out of prison. I don't have to live with that fear anymore."

"I'm so glad you're happy, Josh."

"Carlo said you were worried I wouldn't be happy about it. How could anyone not be?"

"Well, Zin said he didn't take it so well. He felt like he couldn't live the way he wanted to."

"That's understandable. But what we're being given is far better than anything I could have expected. Think about everything I'll be able to do. I'll have forever to see every inch of the world. Maybe someday I'll explore other planets. Who knows? I'm so happy to be alive, Nic. And it's all because of you."

"It's because of Carlo, not me."

"If Carlo didn't care about you so much, he never would've changed me. It's not like he goes around to hospitals changing everyone he sees."

Obviously Carlo didn't think it was necessary to tell him the truth—that I said no to changing him. Another thing I should thank him for.

"I guess he told you what you need to do to stay alive."

"Yeah. We absorb a damaged soul into ourselves."

"Are you okay with that?"

"It's not like we're grabbing people off the street. He told me the person would be at the point of death. What's the alternative for a damaged soul?"

Which is the million-dollar question.

"I hope it doesn't bother you that I'm going on about this," he says. "It's new, you know? I don't want to make you jealous. You're going to live a long, natural, wonderful life, Nic. I'm sure of it."

"I'm not jealous."

But I recognize my words for what they are: a lie. The question is—what am I going to do about it?

WHISPERED WORD

It's a relief to go to Evermore that night, because I've spent hours trying to answer Josh's questions about the Jiang Shi, and none of my answers are good enough for him. That's the thing about Josh—when he wants to know something, he wants to know everything all at once, and pursues it tirelessly.

I arrive at Evermore five minutes after my shift starts and get right to work without chatting with Zin or anyone else. But Zin is watching me, and when I bring back my first order, he asks, "How'd Josh take the news?"

"Good. Great, actually."

He looks surprised. "Really?"

"Yeah. He's elated, like he's been given the world."

"Wow, he can roll with the punches, that guy."

He fills my order, and I bring it to my customers. I was half expecting him to remind me of my promise to come over later. But he doesn't have to—he knows I haven't forgotten.

Carlo greets me with a nod but doesn't approach me. I suppose he's trying to give me space, but the look in his eyes is urgent, even more so than last night.

Since Rambo told me earlier that the Toprocks weren't showing up tonight, I decide to go outside on my break to get some air and watch the usual lineup drama.

"How's it going tonight?" I ask Mig and Richard.

"It's going," Richard replies. I laugh, because it's so not the usual thing he would say.

"They're keeping us busy," Mig says. "We just had to reject a belligerent bunch and they were none too happy."

"I guess you expect a letter to the manager, huh?"

"Yeah." He seems distracted. "It's cold out. You should go back in."

"Okay . . . see you later."

I go back inside, a little hurt that Mig wasn't up for a chat. But I know he's busy, and I shouldn't take it personally. The lineups are full of drama these days, so I shouldn't be distracting them. I might as well use the bathroom, then go back to work.

I hear gunshots.

Chaos swirls around me. I push myself flat against the wall as a horde of screaming people runs in through the front doors.

The music stops, and a cacophony of shouts and shrieks

rings out through the club. Everyone scrambles as far from the front doors as possible. Some escape through the back door.

I run out front to find a small cluster of people on the sidewalk surrounding Mig, who's bleeding profusely. I realize they are all Jiang Shi.

Carlo lifts Mig effortlessly, all two hundred and fifty pounds of him, and slips around the back of the building, heading for the office.

I turn to Zin. "He'll be okay, right?"

"Yeah. We've got to clear people out of here. Let me know if you see the cops."

Zin, Richard, and I have a job to do, and we do it. We go back into the bar, trying to calm people down and guiding them out the back and side doors without letting them trample one another. Meanwhile, my mind is spinning. I bet the group Mig had refused entry to came back seeking revenge. Thank God no one got caught in the crossfire.

It dawns on me that Mig must've guessed that they might come back, and that's why he sent me inside. If I'd been out there one minute later, standing beside him . . . then I would have regretted not letting Carlo change me into a Jiang Shi right away.

I focus on crowd control. Within minutes we have the bar cleared of everyone, including those people who were huddled in the bathrooms, change room, and balcony.

I spot Carlo and Richard at the front of the building, talking to the police. I wonder how they are explaining the blood on the sidewalk if they can't produce a gunshot victim.

In the office, Mig is lying on the couch, his face contorted in pain, while Viola kneels beside him, pressing blood-soaked towels to his torso. He doesn't look so immortal.

Zin puts his arm around me. "He'll be all right. You'll see. Even if we just left him like this for a few days, he'd heal naturally. But Carlo has come up with a much quicker way to heal a Jiang Shi."

He goes to Mig's side. "How many times have you been shot in the last century—five?"

Mig groans. "Fuck you. I didn't ask for this."

"I told you bartending was easier."

I see the corner of Mig's mouth pull up as if he's trying to smile, but instead he grits his teeth. "Can we get started already?"

"Carlo will be back in a minute," Zin says. "He's handling the cops."

The office door opens, and Daniella hurries in. "Mig, not again!" She runs up to him and kisses his forehead.

Moments later Carlo and Richard come in, removing their jackets and rolling up their sleeves. "Ready?" Carlo asks everyone.

The Jiang Shi gather in front of the couch. I hang back,

but Carlo gestures for me to come closer. "You must watch, Raven."

I stand behind the couch as Viola peels the towels off him. There are two gaping wounds—one near the center of his chest, the other in his left abdomen. Carlo passes his hands over Mig's skin with no hesitation or horror, even as the blood flows over his hands. And he starts to list off: "Three shattered ribs, collapsed right lung, hemorrhaging in lower chest cavity . . ."

I try to take it all in. These injuries probably would have been fatal for a mortal. And yet there's no sorrow in this room, only resolve.

Carlo places the hands of the Jiang Shi on different parts of Mig that need healing. Zin's hands are above the shattered ribs, while Viola's are sunken into his chest wound. When everyone has their position, Carlo says, "Now."

Carlo's light appears first, flooding Mig's chest. The lights from the others pour into Mig, and his dark brown eyes fill with white light. His expression goes from anguish to wonder.

Time passes. The Jiang Shi do not move or speak or falter. Their light fills Mig and the room.

Abruptly Carlo lifts his hands, his light vanishing. And one by one the others remove their hands. The glow of light in the room fades, and now there's just a bunch of blood-soaked, exhausted people.

I am in awe. I've witnessed the power of souls to heal, and it's the most incredible thing I've ever seen.

"I need a shower," Mig grumbles, sitting up.

"We'll need a new couch," Daniella says. She's already gotten a mop and is cleaning the floor around the couch.

Zin is in front of me. He wipes away my tears with his thumbs. "You okay?"

I nod.

Now I know what my decision will be.

Zin takes my hand as we walk. I feel so buoyed with love that I'm not sure my feet are touching the ground.

When we get inside his apartment, Zin heads right to the bathroom to peel off his bloody clothes and shower. I sit on the couch, feeling almost giddy as my mind replays Mig's miraculous healing.

Zin emerges with a bath towel wrapped around his waist. It isn't the first time I've seen him shirtless, but it startles my system anyway. His eyes meet mine for a brief moment before he goes into his bedroom and closes the door. He comes out soon after in shorts and a T-shirt.

Sitting down on the couch, he turns to face me. For a second I think he might kiss me, but he just looks into my eyes. I feel my soul rise up to meet his. "Nic. Sweet Nic."

He leans in to kiss me, but I'm smiling so much it interferes.

"I'm so happy we're going to be together," I say. "Forever."

He pulls back, a frown between his eyes. "What do you mean?"

I take a breath; now is the time to tell him. "I guess Carlo didn't tell you about his vision."

"What vision?"

"He said I'm destined to become a Jiang Shi."

Zin looks like I splashed him with cold water. "Explain this to me."

"You were right that he was calling me Raven for a reason. He says he had a vision of a raven with a teardrop in her eye decades ago. Apparently it means that a new era is coming for the Jiang Shi, and I'm supposed to be part of it. He's offered to change me."

"You're just going to accept everything Carlo says as the truth? He'd have to bring you to the point of death—you know that, don't you?"

"I know. I don't like to think about that part, but—"

"This is what I was afraid of! He changed Josh, and everything's roses, and now you're agreeing to let him change you. Damn it, Nic, I thought your beliefs were stronger than that."

"I don't know exactly what I believe, Zin, but I believe in the soul. I believe in the healing I just saw. It was so beautiful."

"That's only one part of what we do. Didn't I explain that it's not all sunshine?"

"You did. I know it wouldn't be the easiest life. But Zin, I could've been killed tonight. I was standing outside with Mig one minute before he got shot. What would you think then? Would you be glad I stuck to my mortality?"

"Don't ask me that. It's not fair. You know it would destroy me if anything happened to you."

"Then why are you so against me becoming a Jiang Shi? Is it just because you don't trust Carlo?"

He seems deep in thought. "I haven't heard anything from Gabriel. Which could mean there really are Heng Te out there. Maybe they—" He breaks off, refusing to finish the thought.

"That would mean Carlo has been telling the truth."

"And it would also mean we're all in danger. If the Heng Te catch Gabriel, they could follow his trail back to us. Is that what you want? To live your life always running?"

"At least I'd have a life to protect. When you're mortal, you can't take the next day for granted. Anything could happen."

"You're pretty set on this, aren't you?"

"Yes."

"Tell me something. Do you want to become a Jiang Shi to be with me?"

I sit beside him, putting a hand on his back. "It's part of it. Isn't it what you want?"

I feel his back tighten against my hand. "I can't guarantee what I'll want a few years from now."

I draw back, pain slashing my insides. So that's how he sees us. Temporary. Whether I'm mortal or not. And I thought he wanted me forever.

I get up to leave, and I'm reminded of another night he rejected me here on this couch. *I'm doing the right thing for you*, he said. But the truth was, he only pushed me away to protect me. And that's exactly what he's doing now.

I sit back down. "So be it, then. If we don't last, we don't last."

He lifts his head. "I'm sorry. I didn't mean that."

"I know."

A look of determination fills his eyes. "I didn't want to do this, Nic—I didn't want to have to tell you why I don't want you to be one of us. But you're giving me no choice."

I swallow. "Tell me then."

"I'll show you."

"What do you—"

But it's too late for questions. His palms are pressed to the side of my head, hot against my skull. He's staring into me, his eyes burning like match flames. "Put your hands on my head, like I'm doing to you."

I place my hands on either side of his head, looking into his eyes. Within seconds I can see his soul in all its brilliance.

Suddenly I'm falling into it, sliding down a wormhole inside him.

I blink, and I'm in a place of darkness. Cold and frightening. I huddle into myself, wishing myself away from here. It's not a quiet darkness. Screams come at me, almost shattering my eardrums, goading me, tormenting me. I try to run, but the walls catch me with strong arms. I'm trapped. A scream of panic rises in my throat.

"Let me out!"

And now I'm on the couch again, sobbing. Zin's arms are around me.

"W-what was that? Where was I?"

"You were inside me."

"But I thought your soul . . ."

"Was a place of light. It is, partially. But inside it, there's a dark place. A place that's created when you take your first soul. I'm not talking about a small tear, or a void, like most people have. I'm talking about a whole room. A place where rage and chaos live."

"You . . . live with that?"

"Every day. That place calls out to me, Nic. Tries to drag me in. In my dreams, I go there almost every night. We all do." He holds my gaze. "You can't trap souls inside you and keep your own soul intact. They rip a hole in you."

"Can't you stop them?"

"No. They keep at you until they weaken your own soul. You need to take another one to restore its energy. It works for a while, until the new soul joins the others and rebels."

I'm still shaking. I don't want to think about him dealing with that place every night. I don't want to think about Josh having to know that place.

He lifts my chin. "Look at me, Nic. Nothing would make me happier than to have you with me forever. But not at the expense of your soul. Do you understand?"

I nod, still shaking.

SHADOW

Josh taps his foot as we ride the subway toward Carlo's. "I feel like a kid meeting his adoptive family for the first time."

He looks so clean-cut and handsome, it's still hard to believe it's really him. His dark brown hair is wet from the rain, his eyes clear and blue. He's wearing a khaki spring jacket, a button-down shirt that matches his eyes, and dress pants—probably one of the outfits Mom bought him in high school for Debate Club competitions.

It's still drizzling when we get off the subway, so we hurry across the street to Carlo's building, huddling under my umbrella. The doorman lets us in and we take the elevator up to Carlo's apartment.

"Swanky building," Josh says. "Looks like Carlo's doing well with Evermore."

"I'm sure he is. Who knows how much you can put away in a few centuries?"

Daniella greets us at the door, taking our coats and leading us into the living room. This is a Jiang Shi Only night, with no mortals but me. Their eyes are fixated on Josh.

Carlo says, "I present to you Joshua, the newest member of our family."

Warmth rises up in the room as everyone gets up to give Josh hugs, handshakes, or European cheek kisses. Zin is the last one to come up. He gives Josh a bear hug and a slap on the back. "Welcome to the family, brother." I know Zin means it. He'll think of Josh as his brother. He'll take care of him.

Josh and I sit on a love seat while Zin balances on the arm beside me, his hand resting on my shoulder.

Across from us on the couch, Richard leans forward. "We met before under different circumstances. Do you remember?"

Josh flushes. "I remember."

"So what's your story?" Daniella wants to know. "Carlo won't tell me anything."

Josh squirms in his seat. "I was a drug addict. I OD'd. Carlo came to the hospital, saved my life."

Okay, so it's out there. It's on the table. But the Jiang Shi aren't done. They have questions. Part of me wants to grab Josh's arm and run. Weren't most of these people from a time when politeness was everything? They have the tact of a wrecking ball.

I glance at Carlo, who is watching all of this with satisfaction. I get it. Josh is one of the family now; there must be no secrets among them.

Carlo looks at me, and I know he's thinking that I'll be the next one to join the family. But I'm not sure anymore. Not after what Zin showed me last night.

Finally the Josh inquisition is over, and the conversation flows into other topics. Josh whispers to me, "Trial by fire."

"You did great. You've got a clean slate now."

He nods. "Tabula rasa."

At dinner the atmosphere is jovial, and Josh enjoys himself, busting his gut laughing at Mig's obnoxious jokes. He's taken my advice not to assault the Jiang Shi with dozens of questions, but he manages to slip in a few well-placed ones, and he cleverly asks for stories that will give him some of the answers he's looking for.

Once dessert is finished, people carry their conversations and teacups back to the living room. I help Carlo gather up the dishes, and so does Zin. I'm not sure if Zin is just being helpful or trying to keep Carlo and me from having a moment alone.

"Your brother is adjusting well," Carlo says.

"He is. It's a relief."

"I told you, there was no reason to worry. Immortality is a gift."

I notice the tension in Zin's jaw, but he doesn't interrupt our conversation. He keeps on loading the dishwasher.

"Any word from Gabriel, Zinadin?" Carlo asks.

Zin answers without turning around. "No. None of us have heard from him."

Carlo knows. I don't know how, but he knows. Maybe he sees in our souls that we know more than we're saying. Maybe it was obvious all along.

"I hope he finds what he's looking for," Carlo says.

Zin slowly turns around. "Just say it. You know why he left, don't you?"

Carlo's face is impassive. "He needed answers that I could not give him. Maybe Gabriel has found the truth already. Maybe he had to die to find it."

Zin stiffens. "You think he's dead?"

"I fear it. I know the Heng Te exist."

I touch Zin's arm, wanting to support him, but he pulls away and gets in front of Carlo. "You know everything, don't you? How can you know there's nothing after death? How can you know when you've never died?"

"My beliefs are based on scientific observation. I've seen souls leave bodies and then dissipate. To me, that means they are gone. Is it possible I am wrong? Yes, it is possible."

Zin's eyes are wide. "You're admitting you could be wrong."

"Of course. I do not profess to know all the secrets of the universe. I only know what I have observed, and I have always presented my Jiang Shi with the truth as I know it."

"And you want Nic to change because of this raven dream you had? What if you're wrong?"

"It is a vision, not a dream. And I have never been wrong in that area, Zinadin. Ever." Carlo looks at me. "I see that you haven't made your decision yet, Raven. You must overcome your fear. There's not much time."

So he sees the fear in my soul. I wonder if he knows what Zin showed me.

Carlo turns back to Zin. "If she could see your soul, would she see that you don't want her to change? Or would she see the truth?"

"You never called me back yesterday, Nic," Chen says the next morning at our lockers. "I wanna know what the hell happened at Evermore Saturday night."

"One of the bouncers got shot, right?" Slide says. "My buddy Paul was in line, and he swears it was the big Hispanic one— Mig, I think. But then in the paper it said no one got hurt."

I hate lying to them, but I don't have a choice. "The paper is right. Some guys who got turned away came back and did a drive-by, but no one was hurt."

"I'm telling you, Paul swears that one of the bouncers was bleeding," Slide insists. "Says his friend saw it too."

"I guess Paul and his friend have overactive imaginations. Mig's fine. Drop by this week and see for yourself."

"I'm glad to hear it," Slide says. "Whoever the trigger man was must've been on crack not to hit anybody, but thank God he didn't. Scary, huh? Evermore's the last place you'd expect that shit to go down. There's never any fights there."

"That's because they sniff out the bad guys and keep them out," Kim says. "Which is exactly why this happened. It's crazy to think that most Saturday nights we would've been there."

"I can't believe I missed the action," Chen says. "The one time I'm not at Evermore on a Saturday night, there's major drama. Just my luck."

Kim rolls her eyes. "Most people would call it good luck."

"Well, I'm starved for action, okay?"

She raises a brow. "What kind of action are you taking about?"

They both laugh. Slide and I just shake our heads.

"Oh, we got big news for you," Slide tells me. "We were at the Vice and we ran into the Spinheads. Chen and Spinman almost had it out—you should've seen it!"

"I could've taken his scrawny ass down," Chen says. "But I didn't wanna get charged, so I figured we'd do it the clean way. They're coming to Evermore in two weeks, Saturday night. We battle them at midnight."

"It'll be the rematch of the century," Kim says sarcastically.

"This is serious shit, Kim," Chen snaps.

"I know, honey," she replies, restraining a smile.

"We're gonna have to practice extra," Slide says, looking at me. I nod. Breaking is the last thing on my mind right now, but I know how important this match is for the guys.

I won't let them down.

Chromeo's sounds are pumping from the stereo. I'm dealing up six steps in slow motion. I've got this idea of kicking both of my legs out at the end, like a Russian dancer, and pushing off from my heels. A good idea in theory, but I can't seem to execute it.

"Try it this way." Chen dips to the floor and does the exact move I have in mind flawlessly.

I groan. "My spine doesn't go all wormy like yours."

"Push off with one arm instead of both," Slide suggests. "More momentum that way."

He's right, and I manage to pull it off—sloppily, but it's a start.

"We'll have to do it in sync," Rambo says, practicing the sequence. "Then we can make it into a full Russian dance." He crosses his arms and springs up on his heels. "Dah, dah, dah!"

We dissolve in laughter, everyone but Zin. "I've got some ideas for moves that'll knock the Spinheads out," he says. "Tell me what you think."

He goes through the moves slowly, one after the other. There's magic in them, but it's not the superhuman magic of before. It's simply the magic of Zin, who can make any move beautiful.

When he's finished, we debate which moves will work best and how to use them. Slide puts on the music and we demo certain parts. Zin works with Chen on the more complex moves that they'll perform together.

It hits me that I'm privileged to be here with these guys, who are so passionate about what they do. But how long will the Toprocks last before life takes everyone in different directions? The thought of it saddens me. I've known better times with these guys than I've ever known before and might ever know again. I just want to grab onto these moments and not let the world, or time, touch them.

But time always changes things. People get older, evolve.

I sense Zin watching me. He probably knows I'm lost in thought, since my moves have slowed down. I can never think and dance at the same time. That's one of the great things about dancing—it temporarily frees me from my thoughts.

I know that Zin will keep his distance until I've given Carlo my decision. And I know it's because Zin is worried that the more attached I am to him, the more likely I'll be to change, despite his warnings. The irony is that it makes no difference whether I have alone time with Zin or not, because I'm already beyond attached to him. He's in my soul, and I'm in his.

He knows that too.

GHOST

"What are you doing?" I ask, watching Josh slide four hundred pounds onto the bar above the bench press.

"I can do it." He winks.

"Yeah, and people might notice. What are they going to think when a guy who's one-seventy benches this kind of weight?"

"Hey, I'm one-seventy-seven. But point taken." He removes two hundred pounds from the bar. "Spot me, will ya?"

"Fine." Me spotting him is a total joke. "Don't do that again when I'm not around, all right? I'm serious about attracting attention."

Getting into position, he lifts the weight easily. "I know. I don't need scientists poking at me or juice monkeys asking for my secret. Maybe I'm trying to send out a message—in case there are any Heng Te around."

"You know?"

"Of course. Carlo told me."

"Are you worried?"

"Not really. I'll be careful. There's one thing I'm sure about." Finishing his first set, he sits up. "I'm not leaving this earth until I'm good and ready. Grandpa told me so."

"Grandpa?"

"He came to me at the very end, just before Carlo showed up. He said it wasn't time for me to cross over."

"You're joking."

"No. I can't say for sure it was real, but I think it was. It wasn't like he came to me while I was dreaming. There was no dream. It was darkness. As far as I know, I was brain-dead then. But I saw him, heard him as clearly as I'm hearing you now."

"What else did he say?"

He lies back down and continues lifting. "He said I won't leave this earth until I've faced my demons. So I figure I've got plenty of years left, even with the Heng Te around."

"You really think it was Grandpa?"

"I do. Carlo thinks it was just my subconscious. He's an atheist, you know. He doesn't believe in God or an afterlife."

"What about you? Do you still believe in God?"

"Anyone would after experiencing a miracle. And that's what it was, even if Carlo calls it science. I think there could well be something after we die, Nic. I respect Carlo, but I don't see how one person could have all the answers."

"So do you feel like maybe you missed something by not crossing over?"

Set done, he sits up again. "I wasn't ready to cross over. Hell, if I'd died, I'd probably be a ghost right now, haunting some idiot with a Ouija board. Or I'd be dead as a doornail. I just know it wasn't my time. It wouldn't have been right for me to die that way, with so much guilt, so much unfinished business. It would've been a total waste. Are you okay?"

I almost let you die that way. I'm so sorry. But I don't think he'd understand my reasons, and I can never tell him.

"I'm fine. Cardio time?"

"Sure, but not too much. I want to keep the poundage I'm putting on. Let's row for ten minutes."

We go to the rowing machines, side by side on the floor. I pull at it hard, slide back and forth, and again.

"You've got lots of energy," he remarks. "Are you sure you're not one of us?"

I grunt. Part of me wants to cry out in frustration. He has no idea what I'm going through right now, how torn I am.

"Mom and Dad seem to be doing well these days." He's rowing at a leisurely pace. "Do you think they're scared I'll relapse?"

"They're definitely scared, but they're good at hiding it. They *are* happy, though. I haven't seen them this way in a long time."

"That's good, because I won't be nearby forever. It'll be nice to know that you'll be around to take care of them. We leave in four years, Carlo says."

"I've heard."

"I have to admit, I'm excited to move on to the next place. And the next. Last night I was up till four in the morning studying maps of the world."

"Did he tell you what the Jiang Shi do in these places?"

"Of course he told me. He said their stop here in New York is like a two-week vacation for them. The next place they hit will be somewhere they're really needed. I think it's great. I always wanted to save the world."

I'm aware of a twinge of hurt inside me. I was hoping he might be thinking about ways he could stay with us longer. Instead he's ready to take off with the Jiang Shi any day. But that's Josh, and it always has been. Once he gets an idea in his mind, it's all he thinks about.

"Oh, and I meant to tell you: I broke it off with Emily. We weren't officially back together, but it was heading in that direction. I made it clear that I had to pursue my own path, and that we didn't have a future." Seeing my expression, he frowns. "What is it? I did the right thing."

"I just feel sad for her."

"Me too. All of us Jiang Shi have to hurt loved ones this way. It's unavoidable."

"I know."

"I know you know." He stops rowing suddenly and turns to me. "To tell you the truth, it pisses me off that Zin let it get to this point with you. I can see the love between you guys. Nothing good can come of it."

He's right. It will end in heartbreak for both of us unless I become one of them.

"I wish you could get away from him as soon as possible, Nic. Start the healing process. If you stay with him for the next four years, it's only going to be worse when he leaves."

"I know."

"But you're not going to let go, are you?"

"It's too late to let go. Can't you see that in my soul?"

He sighs. "I guess I can."

Friday night, past three a.m. It's just Carlo and me in his office.

"You've thought about my offer, I take it?" he asks.

"Yes, and I've decided that I'm not going to let you change me."

"Why?"

"Because I'm not sure. And I think when you're not sure, you shouldn't do something drastic."

I'm waiting for him to comment on my unsophisticated reasoning, but he only says, "Then you are putting your destiny in the hands of fate."

"My destiny has always been in the hands of fate, hasn't it? If something happens to me tomorrow, and you have the opportunity to change me, then do it. But otherwise I'm staying the way I am."

"And what about Zinadin?"

"What about him?" If he wants to challenge my love for Zin, fine.

But he doesn't dare. The truth is right in front of him.

"I think you are making a mistake, Raven. But I respect your decision. My prophecy will unfold regardless. I hope you are prepared."

"I'm not prepared for anything. And I'm not particularly brave, either. So if the prophecy calls for someone like me, I don't understand it." I get up. "I've gotta go."

As I walk to the door, he says, "It won't be easy to return to your regular life when you know what destiny lies ahead of you."

I have no answer for that, so I shrug, then close the door behind me.

Outside the office, Zin is waiting. Without a word, he pulls me into a hug, and I feel my soul mingle with his.

It's useless trying to shake off Carlo's warning. The truth is that I know something is coming. My intuition knows. My dreams, full of ravens, know.

I'm awakened from sleep by a knock at my window. My room is the gray that precedes dawn.

I slip out of bed and pad to the window, looking in between two blinds.

It's Zin. I open the window, and he slides in without a sound. I catch his scent, warm, spicy, and want to carry him back into dreamland. But the distress on his face sobers me.

"I had a dream." He's out of breath, like he's been running.

"Tell me." I take his hand, and we sit down on my bed.

"He's dead." His eyes are full of sadness. "It's my fault. I never should have let him go."

"Oh my God. Gabriel?"

"Yeah. He came to say good-bye."

Shivers go through me. "But it was a dream."

"It was so real. And it explains why I haven't heard from him. I've had this feeling in my gut that something was wrong, from the beginning."

"Did he say how it happened?"

"No. He just said that he was right."

"About what? About Carlo?"

"I took it to mean that he was right about life after death. This dream, this communication . . . it could be the proof, Nic. There *is* something after we die."

"Josh said our grandpa came to him when he was dying. That could be proof too."

"Gabriel's gone. I didn't want to believe it. I wanted to think there was some way he could still be alive. You know what this means, don't you? The Heng Te are real, and they caught up with him."

"If he is dead, then it means he's crossed over to where he wants to be. It means he's solved the mystery. And how do you really know it was the Heng Te? Maybe there's another way for a Jiang Shi to move on that you don't know about."

"Maybe."

"Did he say anything else?"

He looks at me, his eyes haunted. "He asked me when we're going to stop running."

We don't move for a while.

Gradually we lie down, holding hands. We stare at the darkened ceiling as if the answers are written there, if we could only see them.

MIDNIGHT

The Spinheads stride through the doors of Evermore like gunslingers in the Wild West.

We, the Toprocks, are ready.

I quickly change in the back. When I come out, Carlo is there. "A battle tonight, I see. Could you stop by my office when it's over?"

If he's going to say more about how I'm supposed to become a Jiang Shi, I don't want to hear it. But he's the boss, so I nod.

"Good luck, Raven."

"Thanks."

I hit the dance floor. The Toprocks' energy pumps me up. We like to start the battles, so we have to act fast. As a group, we cross the dance floor. Slide steps in front of Spinman and starts doing the monster dance from the "Thriller" video. We laugh.

Spinman gets all puffed up. He never could take a joke. He takes three steps, making a square, then hits the floor with six steps, twisting up on his right arm in a sideways L-kick. Nice.

Zin bursts into the middle with a front flip, landing in the splits. The crowd cheers. He uses his arms to hoist himself up, then spins like a gymnast doing the floor exercise.

Jam knee-drops in, doing multiple windmills. I'm in next with some freestyling. I feel the crowd with me. Dropping to the floor in a worm, I pop up like a jack-in-the-box, then slink back into applejacks, inspiring hoots and cheers.

The Spinheads' girl comes in with two-steps, followed by baby swipes. Not a power move, but good technique. I clap for her, and she glares at me. Another of their b-boys, a new member of Spinman's crew, comes in with broncos, but he's got too much adrenaline, making it impossible for him to keep his legs in the air very long.

You can tell that at this moment Spinman is not loving his crew. We've got to capitalize on that and show a united front of skill. Zin's thinking the same as I am. He dives in and does the new move I made up—which we call the Russian pop-up—with incredible charisma. We all drop to the floor and join him. Each time we pop up, Zin ends the move with a flourish—a backflip, an L-kick, an airswipe. It comes together like we were born to it.

The crowd goes crazy.

We've left the Spinheads in the dust.

The Toprocks pound palms. We'd like to do the same with

the Spinheads, but they're stalking off the dance floor. Sore losers. Well, I can't blame them—we were the same way.

I look around, hoping Carlo saw our victory, but I don't see him. I head for the office but find the door closed. I guess he's waiting for me.

I knock. When there's no answer, I open it, and stop dead.

Carlo is shaking violently as bursts of light stream out of him and rise into the air. Someone is behind him, hands pressed to his head.

I watch, stunned, as the light shapes float up through the ceiling.

"Stop it—you're killing him!"

Carlo slumps on the desk. Behind him, Kim meets my eyes, removing her hands from his head as the last orb of light disappears.

I run to him, shake his shoulders. "Carlo!"

"He's gone," she says softly. "I'm sorry."

"Sorry?" I step away from her. A thousand denials run through my brain. "You killed him."

"Believe me, Nic, I had no choice."

I search her eyes, looking for the person I know. The person I thought was my friend. "Is that you, Kim?"

"It's me."

"You're a Heng Te."

"Yes." She runs to the door and locks it. "I can't believe I forgot to do this. Thank God it was . . . only you."

I realize that she's standing between me and the door.

"Get out of my way," I say, trying to keep my voice from shaking.

To my surprise, she does. "You can leave if you want. But please listen to me first. I need your help."

Is she crazy? I just saw her kill Carlo and now she wants me to help her? I rush toward the door.

"You can save Zin and Josh."

My hand is on the doorknob, but she has my attention. I turn back and face her.

"There are other Heng Te on their way here," she says. "That's why I had to do this tonight. I wanted to give the Jiang Shi a choice before the others arrive."

"What kind of choice?"

"To become mortal."

"Mortal? It's not possible."

"It is. All I have to do is reverse the spell, release the souls they've taken, and leave their original soul intact. The Jiang Shi would go back to the age they were when they were changed and live out their lives like the rest of us."

"Why didn't Carlo have the same choice then?"

"The keeper of the spell had to die. It was the only way to guarantee that no more Jiang Shi are ever created."

"But Carlo had the spell for hundreds of years, and he only changed a few!"

She shakes her head. "Carlo hasn't been honest with you about how many people he changed. There are more Jiang Shi than any of you know. Even if Carlo had promised to never make another Jiang Shi, I couldn't count on him keeping his word. I'm sure it was compassion that motivated him to change the people he did. Compassion is the greatest temptation of all."

I stare at Carlo's lifeless body. I feel like I'm caught in a cloud of dry ice on a dance floor, not knowing which way is up and which is down.

Kim is staring at his body too, with tears in her eyes. "I tried to make it as quick as possible, but he kept resisting. . . ."

Her tears seem real. How can she kill someone one minute and then cry about it the next? It doesn't make sense.

"I don't want this to happen to the others, Nic. If it were up to the Heng Te, they would all end this way. To Heng Te, trapping a soul is worse than murder."

"But they take only diseased souls."

"Even someone with a diseased soul deserves a chance to go to the realm of light. You'd be surprised at the healing that can occur on the other side. Gabriel figured that out."

"Zin thinks Gabriel is dead."

"He's right. His human body is dead. He approached the Heng Te in the Jiangsu province and asked them to release the souls inside him. Despite Carlo's indoctrination, Gabriel had guessed the truth."

"What truth?"

"That death isn't the enemy. That it's just a doorway."

A doorway. It's what I believed before the Jiang Shi came along, before I started questioning everything.

I stare at her, wishing I could see the purity of her soul. She knows that offering to make the Jiang Shi mortal is all I could ever want. It would give Zin and I a chance to spend our lives together. It would give Josh a chance to start over. Kim must know how much I want to believe her.

"Why would you go against the other Heng Te?"

"I've always believed the Heng Te mission was to free souls, not punish immortals. Most of the Heng Te have lost sight of that. I was trained to guide souls to the light, not to hunt down Jiang Shi. When they gave me this mission, I wasn't prepared. I've been in New York for months, and I could never figure out if the group here at Evermore was Jiang Shi or not. The Heng Te are on their way because they're suspicious about why I haven't given a final assessment. They think I've been hiding something . . . which, in these last weeks, I have. When I figured out that the group here was really Jiang Shi, I couldn't give them up."

"How did you figure it out?"

"Zin told us when your brother had been declared brain-dead. Then, a few days later, I find out that he's home with his family. That's when I knew. I didn't tell the Heng Te, but they'll figure it out very soon."

"Will they hurt you?"

"I'll be punished, but it doesn't matter. I have to do this." She looks at me steadily. "Please convince the Jiang Shi to let me turn them into mortals. And if you can't, tell them to run as far and as fast as they can. Because the next time they encounter a Heng Te, they won't get this offer."

It's happened again. In the blink of an eye, the world I know has spun on its axis and settled in a different place.

I walk through the club. The bass beats with the fast, erratic rhythm of my heart. I lean over the bar, grabbing Zin's hand. "Come with me."

I lead him to the balcony, where I sit him down and tell him everything.

He's shaking his head. He doesn't want to believe me.

"It's true, Zin. I saw the souls leave his body."

"No way." He gets up and makes for the stairs.

I hurry after him, but I get caught in the crowd. By the time I get inside the office, Zin is standing over Carlo's body.

I lock the door and walk over to him.

"He's gone." There are tears in his eyes.

"I'm sorry."

"Kim did this? But her soul is pure—I've seen it!"

"She said he had to die so that no more Jiang Shi would be created. He changed a lot more people than just your group."

"Even if he did, he didn't deserve this. We've witnessed horrible things happen to innocent people. Suffering you can't imagine."

"I know. Kim knew it too."

"But she killed him just the same." There's a dangerous gleam in his eyes. "Where is she?"

"I don't know where she is right now. She told me to call her when you've made your decision."

He's staring down at Carlo. "He was right about the Heng Te. I shouldn't have doubted him."

"Don't think about that now. We have to get the others together. You need to decide tonight."

"How do you know Kim won't do this to all of us?" Zin's eyes are still on Carlo. I can't bear to look at Carlo anymore. I can't grieve for him now. There's too much to be done.

"Kim's soul is pure, Zin. You've seen it yourself. And she's giving you a choice. She wants all of you to live."

He's silent for a long time. "You're right. Let's get the others. We can meet in the change room."

"Have you decided?" I hold my breath, my whole world hanging on his answer.

"Yes." His eyes look deep into mine. "I choose you."

◆　◆　◆

It's past two a.m., and the club is still going strong. The part-timers are running the place while the rest of us are gathered in the change room; they think something major is going on, like someone's been caught stealing.

They have no idea.

I look around at the Jiang Shi. "A Heng Te is here. But don't panic—you don't need to be afraid of her. She's here to help. . . . It's Kim."

"Chen's girlfriend, Kim?" Mig's incredulous. "*She's* a Heng Te?"

"Yes. And there are other Heng Te on their way. They could arrive as early as tomorrow morning. Before that happens, she wants to offer all of you the chance to become mortal."

The Jiang Shi stare at me as if I'm insane.

"Is this a joke?" Richard looks around. "Where the hell is Carlo?"

I turn to Zin.

He takes a breath. "There's no easy way to say this. . . . Carlo is dead. Kim took the souls inside him—"

Viola cries out and buries her head in her hands.

"Where is he?" Daniella demands.

"I don't believe it," Richard says. "Carlo was a warrior. He would never have let her get close enough."

"I want to see my brother! Where is he?"

"The office," Zin says.

They rush next door to the office. Zin and I follow.

When the door opens, they gasp. Daniella runs to him first, lifting his head. Then she places it down gently and bends over him, sobbing. Viola drapes her arms over them.

Mig goes over to examine the body. "His light is gone. He's really gone."

"Where's Kim?" Richard shouts. "She'll answer for this!"

"Vengeance against a mortal won't bring him back," Zin says.

Daniella raises her head, her eyes burning into me. "This is your fault! You brought this on us."

"Shh . . ." Mig puts his arms around her. "Nicole wouldn't be able to stop a Heng Te. It's not her fault."

"Yes, it is. She's the raven in Carlo's vision." Daniella's eyes fixate on me. "He knew he was going to die when you showed up. And he was willing to die because he believed it was for a purpose, that you'd lead us to something better. But all you want to do is destroy us. I was right not to trust you. You were supposed to die!" She lunges at me.

Zin grabs her before she can reach me, pinning her arms to her sides.

"What do you mean, she was supposed to die?" A deadly calm enters Zin's voice.

"She should have died. Then all of this wouldn't be

happening. Then Carlo would still be alive!" She struggles in his arms.

"You hired Chris Harris."

"Yes. And I wish he'd succeeded!"

Zin's eyes pulsate. I can see him tighten his grip on her.

"Zin!" I shout.

But it's unnecessary. He releases her and turns away. Daniella begins to sob again.

I can't help but feel sorry for her. What she did, she did out of love for her brother. She probably thought the life of one mortal was more than a fair bargain for that of a Jiang Shi.

Realization dawns. She was right: Carlo must have known he was going to die. And he tried to make me examine the raven's destiny, although he didn't fully understand it himself. My destiny was to signal the new era of the Jiang Shi, but it was never to become one. And the new era was not what Carlo thought—it was the era of mortality.

"I know we all want to grieve for Carlo," I say. "But you have to make your choice soon, before the other Heng Te get here."

"She wants us all dead!" Daniella's voice is shrill. "Look what she did to my brother. And she's the friend of a Heng Te!"

"Kim was my friend too," Zin says. "Neither of us had any idea she was a Heng Te."

Daniella glares at him. "Well, I'm not going along with it. I'm not putting myself at Kim's mercy."

"Me neither," Richard says. "I'm not letting a Heng Te near me."

"I'll go first," Zin offers. "If it doesn't work, you can all be out of town by morning."

"How could you submit to this, Zin?" Daniella asks. "Mortality is nothing but a slow death. You wouldn't agree to this if it weren't for her."

Zin doesn't argue. He just answers, "It's time to stop running."

"I'd rather keep running than grow old and die!" Daniella says. "What kind of a life would that be?"

"A normal life," Viola steps away from Carlo's body. Her face is streaked with tears. "I'm tired of living with no end in sight. The souls inside me want to be released. Sometimes they scream so loud I can hardly stand it."

Mig nods. "I know what you mean. But how do we trust a Heng Te? If we submit to her . . ." He looks at Carlo's body.

"Carlo would be furious that we're even having this conversation." It's Richard. "What's gotten into all of you? Since when are we making deals with the enemy?"

"Kim is not our enemy," Zin says.

Richard scoffs. "She is a Heng Te, and they are responsible for the deaths of Carlo and Martine. For all we know, they could have killed Gabriel, too."

Zin glances at me, then says, "Gabriel gave himself up to them and asked for his souls to be released."

The Jiang Shi look at one another.

"Gabriel is dead?" Viola says.

"Yes."

Daniella snorts. "That's what happens when you submit to a Heng Te. You *die*."

"Gabriel wasn't given the chance that Kim is offering us," Zin says. "She's the only Heng Te who doesn't think we're evil."

"Either way, Carlo would want us to reject this offer," Richard says. "I am not going to accept sixty more years when I can live forever."

"But what if those sixty years are the best you ever live?" Viola asks. "You could settle in one place, get married, have kids. I think it would be . . . wonderful."

"Look around, Viola," Richard says. "A mortal's life isn't as wonderful as you make it out to be. It's suffering, with a little happiness here and there. Why would anyone choose that when you can have immortality?"

"We wouldn't be giving up our immortality," Zin replies. "Gabriel's soul is still alive. He came to me in a dream and asked me when we were going to stop running."

I turn to Josh, who's been stoic throughout all of this. "Tell them about your encounter with Grandpa's spirit when you were in the hospital."

He shrugs. "It could have been a dream."

"But you said it was so clear—that he spoke to you."

He avoids my eyes. "We have no proof of life after death, Nic. All we know is that there's life here and now. Richard is right. I don't want to live just one lifespan, not when I have an option."

"Well, I'm going for it," Mig says. "If nothing else, being mortal will get rid of the noise in my head." He looks at Zin. "And you're willing to go first, to test it out for us?"

"I am."

"Brave kid," Mig says. "So I guess it's time to take a vote. If you're up for the change, stand by Zin. If not, stand next to Richard."

I watch Mig and Viola go over to stand beside Zin, while Daniella links arms with Richard. Josh goes to Daniella and Richard.

I rush over to him. "Please, think about this."

"I have. This is where I belong."

"You belong with your family! You're being given a chance to have a normal life. Don't you want to be with Emily? And be there for Mom and Dad? If you live this way, you'll always be running. You can't really want that."

"I don't want to leave you guys. But if I let her change me, I'll become an addict again. I'd rather die than go back to that."

"It doesn't have to be that way. Even if you did relapse, we'd be there to help you."

"You were there last time and it wasn't enough. It won't be this time, either."

My eyes flood with tears. As much as it hurts, I know he's right. I never want him to go back to his addiction. Never.

"It's time to go," Daniella says. She walks over to Carlo, kisses the top of his head, and whispers something to him.

"Good-bye, Nic," Josh says.

I hug him tight. I don't want to let him go.

The club is closed now, and Kim has returned. I'm so nervous I can hardly breathe.

"Can I . . . go in with him?" I ask, clutching Zin's arm.

Kim shakes her head. "When the souls inside him are let out, they could try to possess you."

Zin hugs me. "If this doesn't work—"

"It has to work."

"I think it will." He pulls back, looking into my eyes. "But if it doesn't, enjoy your life. Don't be sad for me." Then he whispers in my ear, "If this doesn't work, I'll meet you on the other side."

This sounds too much like a good-bye. "Wait! If you don't think this is going to work, please don't do it."

"We have to try." He looks at Kim, who is watching us with the seriousness of a doctor about to undertake a delicate operation. Then he turns back to me. "Whatever happens, I won't be sorry I tried."

His arms go around me, and I feel enveloped by his love. I kiss him with all of the pent-up emotion inside me.

When he ends the kiss, his irises are completely amber, the brightness of his soul gleaming through his eyes. "I love you," he says. I realize he's backing away.

"I love you."

He turns and follows Kim into the office. The door closes behind them.

I don't want to move or breathe or speak until he walks out of that office again.

I feel Viola's hand on my arm. "He'll make it through."

I manage a nod.

Mig is pacing. "Why can't we hear anything?"

"Be patient," Viola says.

A piercing howl shatters the silence. Light shoots through the cracks of the office door.

"He'll withstand," Viola says, her hand tightening on my arm. "He'll withstand." I'm not sure if she's saying it to reassure me or herself.

Mig stops pacing. "She could be killing him. And we're just standing by!"

"This is what Zin wants," Viola says, and then we hear an agonized moan on the other side of the door.

I shudder.

"I'm going in," Mig says.

Viola pulls him away from the door. "We need to let him complete the process."

"Maybe Mig is right," I say. "We could just take a look . . . to make sure Zin is okay."

"No," Viola says. "It's too dangerous for any of us, especially you. Your soul's trying to surface. If you go in there, you'll be vulnerable to whatever's being exorcised from Zin."

I force myself to be still, even as Zin's cries keep coming. To be still, even as the man I love is fighting for his life.

And then there is silence.

ANGELS

It's nearly dawn when Zin and I enter his apartment.

I can hardly grasp that he's mortal, that we can be together for the rest of our lives. I am so close to being completely happy. But then I think of Carlo being dead and what lies ahead for Josh.

Zin looks exhausted, but he's still smiling.

"Are you hungry?" I ask.

He shakes his head. "I have to crash. Guess I haven't adjusted to my mortality yet." I can see the shadows under his eyes. "Will you stay over? I promise I won't get fresh."

I kiss him. "I'll leave a voice mail for my parents."

Zin heads straight for the bedroom. I join him a couple of minutes later, finding him lying across his bed, still in his clothes.

I spread the duvet over him and crawl in.

"Love you," he mumbles.

I curl against his side. "I love you, too."

Within moments I feel myself slipping.

I dream in gray. Of Zin as a tumbler in a carnival of old. Of crowds cheering as he twists and flips. Of him standing, arms outstretched, under the shattering stars of the universe's birthday. Of him slipping out of my arms down a wormhole in the Milky Way, so far I can't reach him. I wake up to the sound of him coughing.

I touch his shoulder. "Are you okay?"

He doesn't reply. He's facing the other direction. I can hear the rattle of his lungs as he tries to breathe.

"Can I get you some water?"

He turns his head, and my heart stops. His skin has a grayish hue, his eyes are mostly closed. He coughs into his hand and curls it up, but not before I see the blood.

I ride to the hospital with him, praying hard.

The EMTs ask me if he's taken any sort of drug. I can only say no. They want to know about pre-existing conditions. They want to know his medical history. What can I tell them? Zin has been in perfect health since I've known him, except that one time when he was adjusting to a new soul.

"Could be pneumonia," the EMT says. "Can take a healthy young person from ten to zero in a few hours."

I'm afraid to ask what number Zin is on that scale. He looks pale, sunken. Like he's lost thirty pounds overnight. Like Josh when he was close to the end.

I look at the EMT. "He told me he once got really sick, back in his home country. It was never diagnosed, but he thought it was tuberculosis."

"Shit!" The EMT reaches for a face mask.

The white hospital halls, with their fluorescent lights, are a labyrinth of nightmares. If there is a purgatory, this would be it. Any moment a door can open with an announcement of death.

Zin is under quarantine. I can only see him through the glass in the door, and even then, there are all these machines in the way.

Touch and go. It's too soon to know if the antibiotics will work.

I keep hoping I'll turn around and Carlo will be there. If Zin doesn't recover, Carlo would've been able to save him.

But Carlo is gone.

I take out my cell phone, call Viola, get her voice mail. I call Mig. His girlfriend answers.

"Hey, it's Nicole. Is Mig there?"

"He's in the hospital. They're telling me he has blood poisoning. I have no idea how it happened."

Oh my God.

All of them. It's happening to all of them.

And it's my fault. I convinced them to change without thinking of possible consequences. Even Kim must not have known.

I should've told them to run. I shouldn't have let them take the risk.

What have I done?

Zin's words echo in my mind. *Some of us have more than we deserve. And if there's any justice in this world, we'll have to pay for it.*

On the fourth day the doctor tells me that Zin's taken a turn for the better.

I want to cry with relief. The doctor starts to walk away, but I catch his sleeve. "Can I see him?"

"No. He'll be in quarantine at least two more days."

Fine. I can wait. I'll wait for days or weeks, as long as Zin is okay.

He can see me through the square of glass in the door. I wave. He gives a weak smile.

I press a paper against the window. I LOVE YOU.

Mig's arms are outstretched, and I walk into them. We're outside of Viola's hospital room.

"Are you ready to see her?" he asks.

"Not yet. Is she really as bad as you said? Are you sure she can't go into remission?"

"I'm sure. We won't have her for much longer. Go on. She's been asking for you."

I want to burst into tears. "I'm not sure if . . ." Maybe I shouldn't see her. Maybe she'd want me to remember her in her beautiful days, not sickly and near death.

But no, I'm not going to be a coward. I do want to see her. "I'm ready."

I walk into the room. The sight of her is a shock, but I force myself to smile. Viola has wasted away to little more than a skeleton. Her blue eyes are protuberant in her sunken face. Her skin is almost translucent.

Carlo saved her from this once. And she loved him forever.

When she sees me, her eyes flicker just enough to register surprise. "Nic." Her hand reaches out to grasp mine.

"Hi, Viola."

Her voice is a weak rasp. "Does being mortal always feel this shitty?"

I smile, but I can only think of how unfair it is that Viola has ovarian cancer, a disease that modern medicine has yet to conquer, while Mig and Zin have recovered.

"I wish Zin could be here too," I say. "He's still under quarantine. I guess they told you."

"Tell him I love him."

"I will."

The tears are rising inside me, but I won't release them. I don't want to cry for her before she's gone.

"It's okay if you have to cry," she says gently.

I tremble as tears flow out of my eyes. "S-sorry."

"Don't be." There's strength in her frail hand. Amazing, but I feel like she's holding me up.

"I hope you forgive me. I didn't know this would—" My voice breaks.

"There's nothing to forgive. We knew something like this could happen. It was worth taking a chance."

I don't know if she's just being kind, or if she really doesn't have regrets.

"Could you pass me the water?"

I hold up the glass and fit the straw between her lips. She sucks it for a few moments. "Don't be sad, Nic. I've had a good three hundred years. I'm not afraid to die."

"Really?"

"Yes." Her smile is radiant, and for a second I recognize the old Viola. "I have a feeling Carlo's waiting for me. And you know he doesn't like to be kept waiting."

"Is it the universe's birthday again?" I ask, stepping out onto the roof. The night tastes of Hudson breeze and city smoke.

"The universe can't have a birthday twice in one year.

Tonight is something totally different. Let's call it an inter-planetary party."

I laugh. "As long as I'm invited."

Zin grins. "Wouldn't be a party without you."

He pushes two lounge chairs together and we both stretch out, looking up at the stars.

I breathe the night in. If there is a divine force out there, I say to myself, this is how I'd want to speak to it—through the stars.

Thank you for Zin being well. Thank you. Thank you.

"Mortality surprises me, Nic. I've got this quiet inside me. I never thought I'd say this, but I feel totally peaceful. I hope this feeling lasts a long time."

"I hope it does too."

Happy as I am at this moment, I doubt I'll ever totally be at peace. I can't, knowing that Josh is on the run and might encounter the Heng Te. But I'll live with that, because I carry him in my soul. Maybe perfect peace isn't meant to be part of the human condition. Who knows? I only know that I am so grateful to have Zin by my side.

"You should be careful crossing the street," I tell him. "You're not immortal anymore."

"I'm being careful. I'm living in a whole new way because I intend to stick around for a long time."

"You'd better."

We lay there in silence, falling into our thoughts.

"I wonder if Kim will come back," he says eventually. "I'm worried about Chen."

The last time I saw her, she'd just rushed us out of the club after changing Zin, Viola, and Mig. She told us she was going to face the Heng Te, whatever the consequences.

"I hope she gets back soon for Chen's sake, and for the Toprocks," I say. "Chen's lost his fire. We need the old Chen back."

"Yeah. Everything has changed so much, huh?" I can hear the sadness in his voice. "Whenever I walk into Evermore, I keep expecting to see everyone. I still don't think it's hit me."

"I know what you mean. . . . I guess it'll take a while."

I miss the others too, especially Viola, whose spirit was the most beautiful part of her. But I can't imagine how it would be for Zin to lose most of his family in such a short period of time. I know he's grieving, and he prefers to grieve alone. But he knows I'm here when he needs me.

"Mig's doing a good job of running Evermore," I say, changing the subject. "Do you think he's going to keep it going for a while?"

"I think so. He sees it as a way to honor Carlo. And guess what?"

"What?"

"He asked me if I'd manage it with him. Picture me as a manager, and only twenty years old."

"You're way too inexperienced. Maybe in a few years."

I hear him chuckle.

As I look up into the night sky, a feeling of calm spreads over me. And I know that Zin and the stars are more than I'll ever need.

I turn on my side, and we smile at each other. Even in the darkness there is a glow coming from him, a light that burns hot and bright like a lithium battery. That light was never the Jiang Shi. It was always Zin.

DRUGS. DEALS. SURVIVAL.

Street Pharm

GIVING THE DRIVER HIS CASH, I RAN INSIDE THE BUILDING and hit the button. Sonny buzzed me up. He was standing in the doorway of his apartment in sweat pants and a wife-beater. "Get in here."

The apartment was huge, with sleek tiled floors, leather couches, and a hot entertainment system. I barely sat down when Sonny said, "Carlos got jumped tonight when he was making deliveries. They fucked him up, took the stuff, and made him cough up the names of the customers he was delivering to."

"You talked to Carlos?"

"No, his girl called me. Them bitches who messed him up told him to give us a message: 'Darkman's in town and he's shutting us down.'"

"Darkman? He some sorta comic character?"

"Whoever the fuck he is, he knows who we are. Carlos can't hold in a fucking fart."

"*Shit*, I got warned about this."

"Huh? Who warned you?"

"Monfrey. Said there was some shady niggas around. I didn't take him serious."

I was all about Alyse then, I remembered. *Damn*, I was right that women were a distraction.

I said, "Anybody new in the hood can tell that Carlos is probably running for someone. That skinny cat ain't sly. So we don't know how much Darkman knows about us. He could've been lying low for weeks, getting ready to strike."

I heard Sonny swallow.

"We gonna hold it down," I said. "First thing we have to worry about is that he knows the names of some customers. He might try to sweet-talk them into buying from him. We gotta get to them first and let 'em know we still the best deal in town."

"I been all over that. Carlos's girl told me the names of the three customers he gave up, and I spoke to them. They'll get their next hit half price. We cool with them."

"Good, you stay on it. We have to remind our peeps that we still their number one. Keep 'em happy. I'll deal with the other side of this. I'm gonna find out who this Darkman is."

"And then what?"

"We wait for him on the battlefield."

I found Rob Monfrey the next morning on a park bench, smoking up.

"Ty, what it be like?"

"We got trouble." I scanned the bench for bird shit and sat down.

"I know. Heard they fucked up Carlos."

"Uh-huh. Tell me everything you know about this Darkman."

"All I know is, he used to run a big-time operation down in Miami. Don't know why he came up here. The guys working for him, they from Miami too."

"I hope he bought them return tickets. They try to sell to you?"

"Yeah, last night. One of 'em saw me smoking. Asked where I got the stuff. Said I found it in a mailbox. He said he'd sell me some real cheap. I told him I don't smoke regular like. He said, 'Yeah, right,' and walked away."

"I like how you handled that. But next time, do it different. If you stay visible, one of those guys is gonna approach you again. Let 'em know you can't afford to pay for no weed. But if they need shit done, you can swing that."

"Sounds like you asking me to be a spy." Monfrey grinned. "I like it, son."

"Make yourself mad helpful to them. I want you to find out everything you can about their leader and their operation. Find out Darkman's real name, how many men he got working for him, where he goes to eat—anything."

"Easy peasy."

"You a natural, Monfrey, but these guys are dangerous. If you think they suspect you, get away from them fast—got that?"

"I got you."

"You can name your price for this job."

"PlayStation 3?"

That was the thing about Monfrey. He had no fucking idea how much he was worth.

"PlayStation 3, ten of the hottest games, and a pair of Jordans. How about that?"

He slapped my hand. "We got a deal."

I didn't go to school on Monday. No time. I had to secure my ops, and that meant talking to every member of my team, from the big players to the small-time runners, to make sure there weren't any cracks.

I was straight-up with my peeps. We had a competitor and we had to be ready. Since I didn't want to leave anything important on an answering machine, I called each one until I talked to them. I didn't go see them face-to-face. I wasn't gonna make Darkman's job any easier by leading him to my peeps.

My work was just getting started. I stopped by a few choice spots: pool halls, take-outs, barbershops, delis, bars—all places where they knew me. Places where new faces would get noticed. Places where I could ask questions and get the straight-up goods.

I learned enough about my enemy to start a profile of him on my Palm Pilot.

Darkman:

- late twenties
- first name Kevin
- cocky
- Miami Crip connection
- family is big in Miami drug scene
- brought three guys with him from Florida (two black, one Hispanic, probably Cuban)
- has a high-maintenance girlfriend named Leanne

The question bugging me the most was why he was here in the first place. If he was so big in Miami, why did he leave?

Maybe the stories about him being a Florida big shot were made up. Or maybe his family was running the show and he decided to go off on his own. Maybe he came to Brooklyn because he had something to prove.

One thing was for sure: If Darkman thought he could just come to BK and crown himself a kingpin, he was wrong.

I was thinking of all this when I walked through the door at 11:30 that night. Mom wasn't home, lucky for me. I needed to be alone to do some serious planning.

There was a postcard on the kitchen table.

◆　◆　◆

Hey Ty,

How about them Giants? What a great game last night!

I'm missing your letters. Don't forget to write when you get time.

Your dad

Anything about a sports team was our emergency code.
Dad wanted me there ASAP.

One label can
brand you for life.

Friday night. Me and my girls, Q, Marie, Vicky, and Melisha, arrived at the dance twenty minutes after it started. Screw being fashionably late—we wanted to go through security as fast as possible so we could hit the dance floor.

Or, as Marie said, we wanted first pick of the ass.

We'd been a group since junior high, when the five of us ended up in the same class. Q, Melisha, and me already knew one another. Vicky and Marie were newbies from other schools and sticking together. It actually started with a school yard beef; word got to Marie that Q had made fun of her hairstyle in front of some guys. Instead of letting my best friend get jumped, which I heard was the plan, I went to Marie and Vicky to plead Q's innocence. They not only believed me, they gave me props for going up to them and went over to meet Q and Melisha. We'd all been tight ever since. To this day, Q says she never said that about Marie's hair, but knowing Q's views on the importance of good hair, I never believed her.

It's amazing how we all stuck like glue, especially considering Marie was a member of the Real Live Bitches. She got recruited in freshman year, when the RLB was scrambling to counter floods of Crips coming in. They'd tried to recruit all of us that year, but we made them back off by playing innocent and weak, qualities the RLB hated. Marie was the one who got up in their faces, and after fighting some members, she decided to stop resisting her destiny and become a Bitch herself.

Unlike most of the RLB, Marie still hung out with nonmembers whenever she felt like it. In fact, she told me once that the main reason she joined was for a shot at some hot guys. You see, she was mad horny.

To my surprise, the gym was crowded when we walked in. Probably with freshmen, but I didn't care. At least there were people on the dance floor. We hit it immediately, cheesy colorful lights flashing around us.

The music wasn't half bad for a school-hired DJ, though we only heard the clean versions of songs, like Akon's ode to strippers, "I Wanna Love You." We sang along using the real lyrics, and had a good laugh dancing with imaginary stripper poles.

Within an hour the gym filled to the max, and I couldn't help scanning for Eric, cute dean's office guy. I'd promised myself that if he showed up, I'd make a point of talking to him, if only to prove to Q that I wasn't a punk.

I didn't see him. What I saw instead was a bunch of kids displaying gang colors, mostly flags and bandannas they'd smuggled in. I looked at my watch, wondering how much dancing we'd get in before trouble started.

When the DJ got on the mike to do shout-outs, I walked off the dance floor to take a breather and a drink at the fountain. As soon as I caught my breath and reapplied my lip gloss, I'd go back to my friends.

"Hey, I know you," someone shouted in my ear.

He materialized at my elbow, like out of nowhere. He seemed bigger than I remembered, maybe because he wasn't hunched in a chair. Six feet tall at least, with broad shoulders filling out his Pistons jersey. Sean John jeans hung loosely around his legs, held up by a belt with a silver buckle.

I felt a smile coming, but I kept it subtle—no way I was going to let on that I'd been hoping to see him here.

"I know you too. . . ." I said as if I didn't remember his name.

"It's Eric Valienté."

"Julia DiVino."

He leaned closer. "Di-what?"

"*DiVino*. It's Italian. But I'm Puerto Rican on my mom's side."

He smiled. "I didn't know I was messing with no Puerto Rican." He rolled his Rs like he spoke Spanish. Sexy.

I could hear my heartbeat, separate from the music, pounding in my ears. Eric Valienté was giving me sensory overload. We had to stand really close to talk over the loud music, and it was messing with my hormones.

"I'm a mutt too," he said. "Dad's Dominican, Mom's Mexican."

"Nice mix."

"They didn't think so. They got divorced."

That could be a conversation killer if I didn't keep the ball rolling. "I never heard how you ended up in Brooklyn."

"Got into some trouble in Detroit. Nothing big, but my mom thought I should come here for a fresh start. So I'm living with my dad now. How's that for an answer?"

"Okay, except you didn't say what the trouble was."

"Right, I didn't." He winked, then turned his attention to the dance floor.

Shit. Had I said the wrong thing? Did he think I wasn't good-looking from up close? My dad hadn't thought one crooked eye-tooth justified the cost of braces. Probably true, but I cursed him for it anyway. Plus, my skin was giving me problems. I'd dropped ten bucks on oil-free cover-up, and I hoped it was working.

"Are all the teachers here crazy like that one?" he asked.

I spotted Ms. Carter doing some disco moves in the middle of a group of kids. The moves actually went well with the Usher song playing. "Ah, she's just having fun. She's the least crazy teacher you'll find here."

"You playing?"

"I don't play."

He smiled. Yeah, we were feeling each other. I wondered what he'd do if I leaned over and kissed him. Of course, I wouldn't do that. Not unless I were drunk, which I wasn't, unfortunately.

Then somebody grabbed my sleeve.

"Who is *he*?" It was my friend Melisha, her eyelids sparkling with silver glitter.

"I'll tell you later. Now bounce, okay?"

"Fine, but I hope he got friends for the rest of us!"

I turned back to Eric. He was scanning the room. "Lot of people rocking colors," he said.

I sighed. "Yeah. It's mostly a Blood school, but we've got more and more Crips here now. When they closed down Tilson, lots of them came here."

He nudged his chin toward the Crips. "You see what they're doing?"

I saw. There was a group of Crips by the speakers. Two of them were doing the *CripWalk*—a little dance meant to piss off the Bloods.

"Can't they keep that shit out of here?" I looked around, spotting the security guards. They weren't paying any attention. They were flirting with some girls.

"I think something's gonna start," he said. "We better—"

I stopped listening. I watched a guy in a red do-rag walk up to one of the Crip dancers and snuff him right in the face.

Chaos broke out.

I felt Eric grab my arm and drag me through the crowd. Half the people in the gym were running toward the fight, half were running away from it to the main doors. I covered my face against the long nails and elbows as Eric yanked me through the mess of people.

I felt him push me against the wall. But it wasn't a wall, it was a door. It must've been a fire exit. I found myself in the parking lot behind the school. A bunch of kids rushed out after us.

"What the hell is happening?" I tried to catch my breath.

"They're trying to kill each other," he said. "Nothing new. I gotta go."

"Don't!" I grabbed his arm, but he pulled away and disappeared back inside.

Why the hell did he go back in? What was he thinking?

"God, Julia!" Q threw her arms around me. "I was worried you were caught in the middle of that! Somebody got stabbed. Did you see what happened?"

"Bloods and Crips," I said. "That's what happened."

ABOUT THE AUTHOR

Allison van Diepen is also the author of *Street Pharm* and *Snitch*. She teaches at an alternative high school in Ottawa, Canada. Visit her on the Web at AllisonvanDiepen.com or at MySpace.com/allisonvandiepen.

Did you love this book?

Want to get access to
the hottest books for free?

Log on to simonandschuster.com/pulseit
to find out how to join,

get access to cool sweepstakes,

and hear about your favorite authors!

Become part of Pulse IT and tell us what you think!

Margaret K.
McElderry Books SIMON & SCHUSTER BFYR

Psst . . . **Here is our latest secret.**

LISA SCHROEDER

ELLEN HOPKINS

SONYA SONES

Get *In Verse*

A poetry online sampler from Simon & Schuster

Available at TEEN.SimonandSchuster.com

TERRA ELAN McVOY

CAROL LYNCH WILLIAMS

STEVEN HERRICK

Simon Pulse | Paula Wiseman Books
Simon & Schuster Books for Young Readers
Published by Simon & Schuster

Twitter.com/SimonTEEN

simonTeen

Simon & Schuster's **Simon Teen**
e-newsletter delivers current updates on
the hottest titles, exciting sweepstakes, and
exclusive content from your favorite authors.

Visit **TEEN.SimonandSchuster.com** to
sign up, post your thoughts, and find out what
every avid reader is talking about!

Margaret K. McElderry Books

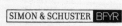 SIMON & SCHUSTER BFYR

SIMON
PULSE